Garry Disher grew up on a wheat and wool farm in South Australia. He has an MA in Australian History and has lived, worked and travelled in England, Italy, Israel, the USA and southern Africa. In 1978 he was awarded a creative writing fellowship to Stanford University, where he wrote his first collection of short stories. Garry worked as a writing lecturer between the years 1980 and 1988, before becoming a full-time writer. He has published over fifty books, including short story collections, literary novels, writers' handbooks and award-winning crime thrillers and children's titles.

LOTHIAN CLASSICS
by Garry Disher

Eva's Angel
From Your Friend, Louis Deane
Good One, Erm
Maddie Finn
Ratface
Restless
The Apostle Bird
The Bamboo Flute
The Divine Wind
Two-way Cut
Walk Twenty, Run Twenty

GARRY DISHER

RESTLESS

LOTHIAN

Acknowledgements

The author and publisher gratefully acknowledge the publications in which these stories first appeared: 'Dead Set' in Gary Crew (ed), *Dark House*, Mammoth Books, Melbourne, 1995; 'Where the Bodies are Buried' in Lucy Sussex (ed) *Shadow Alley*, Omnibus Books, Adelaide, 1995; 'Blame the Wind' in Penny Matthews (ed), *Spine Chilling*, Omibus Books, Adelaide, 1992. 'Poor Reception' and 'The Difference to Me' are significantly reworked versions of stories from the author's second short story collection, *The Difference to Me*, Angus & Robertson, Sydney, 1988.

'lycra' on page 8 is a Trademark

A Lothian Children's Book

This edition published in Australia and New Zealand in 2019
by Hachette Australia
(an imprint of Hachette Australia Pty Limited)
Level 17, 207 Kent Street, Sydney NSW 2000
www.hachettechildrens.com.au

First published in Australia in 1995 by Angus & Robertson
Published in 2002 by Hodder Headline Australia Pty Limited

10 9 8 7 6 5 4 3 2 1

A catalogue record for this book is available from the National Library of Australia

ISBN 978 0 7336 4171 8 (paperback)

Cover design by Grace West
Typeset by Bookhouse, Sydney
Author photograph courtesy L. Healey
Printed and bound in Australia by McPherson's Printing Group

The paper this book is printed on is certified against the Forest Stewardship Council® Standards. McPherson's Printing Group holds FSC® chain of custody certification SA-COC-005379. FSC® promotes environmentally responsible, socially beneficial and economically viable management of the world's forests.

CONTENTS

To Margot, Alexis and Jules

DEAD SET

A paralysing sense of loss and dread seemed to wrap itself around me from the very first morning. I'd feel it when they yanked me out of bed, I'd feel it when I ate the White Feather breakfast (toast, one slice; tea brewed from yesterday's bag), it was there through the long days and nights. I became a morbid reader of the *Herald* because of it — all those murders, riots, train wrecks and bushfires. I should have been saying *See? There are lives worse than mine in the world*, but I couldn't. Something was going to happen, I could feel it, and there was nothing I could do but wait.

On the day that it all started, the *Herald* had this for me: 'BODY FOUND: The partly mummified remains of an elderly woman, concealed in the window seat of a derelict house, were uncovered by workmen in Melbourne yesterday.'

That's all, three lines, no answers, just the bare bones, so to speak. You never get answers in the *Herald*, and this only served to increase my anxiety.

Did she crawl into the window seat to die? Did someone put her there? Did he slit her throat first?

That was as far as I got that morning. A gingery hand slapped me — left, right, across each ear — and the *Herald* was snatched from my grasp.

'Weak shit. Blow-out.'

It was Curtis. I hadn't heard him enter the caravan. Curtis liked surprises; he liked to slink around us like a shadow, a spy.

He was wearing a lilac tracksuit, I remember, with Reebok hightops. His spiky hair was still wet from the shower, and his cricketer's moustache drooped like a joke on either side of his damp, parted lips. But Curtis was no joke. His hand flashed out again and my head snapped back with the pain of it. 'You're a weak shit, Ben. What are you?'

I muttered something. I wasn't about to call myself a weak shit.

He put his hand to his ear. 'Sorry? I didn't quite catch that.'

I stared at him, ready for another blow. The other guys were waiting for it, too, the remains of their White Feather breakfasts at their elbows. It was a six-berth caravan, pretty crowded, and there was no means of escape with old Curtis blocking the way. But at least the others had been working. Their sales kits were spread open on the table — they'd been memorising the seven-page presentation, not reading the morning newspaper.

Curtis stared back at me. Then a change came over his good-looking face, a wide, false grin directed at everyone. 'Guys, loosen up. Let's have some enthusiasm here, okay?'

And we all grinned back at him, chorusing 'okay'. Me, too. I'm prepared to behave like a moron if it'll get me off the hook.

'When you guys go out on your rounds tonight,' Curtis said, 'you're going to sell, sell, sell.'

And we all jumped up and down and whooped like cowboys and punched the air like athletes and shouted, 'Sell! Sell! Sell!'

Curtis held up a hand. 'After tonight,' he beamed, *'no more white feathers!'*

'Yay!'

The white feather signified a wimp, a coward, a weak shit, a blow-out. It meant that you hadn't learnt your sales presentation yet, or, if you had, that you weren't showing *enthusiasm.* It meant that you hadn't sold some poor sucker a set of Colman International encyclopaedias worth $1900, and all you deserved for breakfast was toast, one slice, and tea brewed from yesterday's bag.

'Guys,' Curtis said, 'tonight's the night you break the ice.'

And we jerked around again, enthusiasm written all over us.

Curtis leant forward, serious now. 'Remember what I said about one hundred per cent? Colman International gives a hundred per cent: if you can give a hundred per cent as well, how can we lose?'

'Hundred per cent,' we said solemnly.

'And what did I say the difference was between a mediocre actor and a great one?' He looked at me. 'Ben?'

I recited automatically: 'The great actor knows how to put force and meaning into his lines.'

'Right! And does a great actor ever change the words of Shakespeare? No! The words are there because they work, but they can only work if they are delivered with passion!'

Curtis stepped back after this, folded his arms, let the seconds tick by. I knew all his moves by then. This was the one where he waited for an electric tension to build up. Finally he said softly, 'Guys, it's the same with the Colman International sales presentation — the words won't work for you *unless you deliver them with enthusiasm.*'

And he slipped out of the caravan, into the sunshine, leaving a chill in the air. We looked at one another, dumped our dishes in the sink, and threw ourselves into memorising the sales presentation.

Excitement, travel, and the opportunity to earn up to

$80,000 a year, that's what the advertisement had told me. It hadn't told me I'd be sent to Sydney on a bus. It didn't say I'd be taken to a dreary campground near a freeway, to share a dingy caravan with other homesick kids, other school-leavers desperate for a job. It didn't say I'd be paid only if I made a sale, and that food and accommodation would be deducted from it.

The long day passed. By evening our nerves were ragged. We changed into good clothes and mustered in the car park. Dusk. Mums and dads home from work, little kids in their pyjamas — entire suburbs a sitting target for the guys from Colman International.

There were eighteen of us altogether, in three caravans. For all I knew, we were all White Feathers, but no one admitted to it. Anyhow, part of Curtis's strategy was to take us aside individually and hiss: 'Why is it that the others can make sales and you can't? You blow-out.'

Three minibuses pulled into the car park and we climbed aboard. We were driven through the dark streets. All those houses! All those potential buyers! Curtis was there, whipping up enthusiasm. 'Sing!' he said, and we clapped and shouted. That night it was aimed at me, as usual: 'Go out, Ben, and sell some books, doo-da, doo-da.' I preferred it when we sang, 'I'm going to knock on your door, ring on your bell, sell you some encyclopaedias . . .'

Curtis dropped us off one by one. My starting point

was a dark corner at the entrance to a black and silent street, but that was no burden to a guy from Colman International. I was there to sell! sell! sell!

One hour later I was not feeling so chirpy. So much for enthusiasm — I could feel it draining away as if it were my life's blood. I was supposed to keep a running report for Curtis: address, age and sex of the householders, responses to the sales presentation. Sales presentation? I was barely able to say, 'Hello, my name is Ben and —' before the door was slammed in my face. A three-year-old with no pants on answered at one house. He stared at me, scummed with peanut butter, before his mother snatched him away. At another place an old geezer coughed his lungs out for ten minutes just trying to say hello. Some kids were partying at a block of flats. There was dope in the air and Madonna on at full volume, and they all giggled at me as if I'd come to sell them Jesus. Not that I wrote any of that in my report. Curtis would only have snapped *opportunity missed* and called me a blow-out. I wrote 'No one at home'. There were a lot of people not at home in that area that night.

It was in that frame of mind, with low expectations, that I approached the last house in the street, a brick-veneer like all the others.

But it wasn't the last house. At just that moment, as clouds passed across the face of the moon and a sudden wind agitated the ancient plane tree that had been obscuring the only working street light, I noticed a high stone wall in the shadows beyond. I felt as if I'd come to a forgotten corner of the world and there was one more mystery to encounter. Forget the brick veneer — it was the cobbled lane at the side, the stone wall choked with vines, the impression of a silent, looming shape behind it, that I was interested in. There was a big house in there and I could feel the tug of it, as though it held the answers to everything.

There was no clear way in. I circled the wall, stumbling in the moonlight. The second time around I discovered a gate. It was open a fraction, though I'm sure it hadn't been open the first time. But that was not the kind of thing I wanted to dwell on right then.

I followed a path to the front door. Some front door: there was plenty of weight and authority in it, high, wide and solid, a lion's-head knocker at chin level, stained-glass panels on either side. A door like that wasn't going to admit me to snotty babies, phlegmy old men or dope fiends. There was a light on inside, swimming faint and green behind the stained glass. Then I knocked and I sensed what I can only describe as a relief of tension, as if I'd been expected all along and at last I'd arrived.

The door opened immediately, though I'd not seen or heard anyone in the hallway on the other side. The door opened and I fired up at once: 'Hello, my name is Ben, and I'm in the area tonight talking to people about —'

'Come in,' she said.

The voice was the first thing I noticed. Low, throaty, calm, welcoming, it seemed to say that I mattered. No one had told me that I mattered for a while. Then I noticed her face. In the semi-darkness it was composed of beautifully aligned shapes and shadows. She was about my height, my age.

'Follow me.'

She had the slender, flickering shape of a flame. I followed her through the house, scarcely noticing the other doors in the hallway, the staircase or the silent paintings that watched me go by. We came to a candlelit room and all I wanted to do was curl up in the warmth and half light and listen to that voice and watch the soft lines of that face.

She showed me to a couch and invited me to sit. Then she sat at the other end, folding her long legs beneath her. Black lycra tights, a black top, gold gleaming softly here and there on her earlobes, fingers and throat. Her hair was tousled, her face peaceful and drowsy. She was like a cat.

'Cat,' she said softly. 'Caterina.'

She was there in my head. Creepy. 'Ben,' I said.

She echoed it, *Ben*, like a caress.

I looked away, I had to. It was a high-ceilinged room, soft and restful in the muted light, a grandfather clock beating slowly in the stillness behind me. A room for the calm contemplation of ideas and beauty, and I guess that's what Cat did there. Books, paintings, a music stand, a single cut flower in a fluted vase. She hadn't bothered to draw the curtains over the deep recess of the bay window. There were shapes in the moonlight outside: shrubs, a tree, a ladder, the impenetrable wall beyond.

In another life I'd like to be a filmmaker. There's a trick I do with my eyes sometimes, pulling back from a long focus in stages, as if they were a movie camera. I did it then, pulling back through the window glass into the room.

And my heart stopped.

Freeze frame. She had a window seat. I remembered the morning's headline: *Body Found.*

'It was a love story,' Cat said.

She was listening to my thoughts again. I didn't say anything. All I could do was stare.

'The old woman found in the window seat,' she said. 'It was a love story.'

My voice had better not betray me. 'She wasn't murdered?'

'No.'

'What happened?'

'An old couple used to live there. When the wife died, her husband couldn't bear to be parted from her, so he put her in the window seat. Several years went by and then one day he died, sitting on a park bench in the sun. No one knew he had a wife.'

Good. I was glad it was a love story. Time went by in that comfortable room. The candle flickered, and I didn't mention Colman's encyclopaedia. I didn't ask Cat how she knew the answer to the problem of the body in the window seat. I'm not even sure that we said anything aloud to each other. It was as if her voice was there in my head and mine was in hers.

Then a man crossed the room behind her and I came out of my dream. He was young, vigorous, in a hurry, drawing on white gloves, an ebony cane under his arm. It wasn't fair. I wanted Cat to myself.

'Mr Dysart,' Cat said.

I looked at her. She was grinning. There was no malice in it. 'Mr Dysart lived here at the turn of the century. He was in such a hurry one evening that he slipped, hit his head, and died.'

She was telling me that I had the gift of seeing and knowing what others couldn't. A lot of things made sense suddenly: feelings I'd been having, pictures in my head. Coming to that house and meeting Cat was like coming home, like finding a missing part of myself.

I looked at my watch. Almost nine p.m. and I was supposed to rendezvous with Curtis at ten. No sales, and I hadn't covered half the houses in the area assigned to me.

'I don't need encyclopaedias,' Cat said, indicating the bookshelves behind her.

'I know.'

'But I'll buy the *Almanac.*'

The *Almanac* is a book of months and days of the year, full of quirky astronomical information. We were not supposed to sell it separately. It was supposed to be a special, never-to-be-repeated offer to anyone who bought a set of encyclopaedias.

I grinned. 'Okay.'

Maybe it would keep Curtis off my back. I could show him my report — 'Sold, one *Almanac*' — and he'd clap me on the shoulders and pump my hand and never call me a weak shit again.

Cat showed me to the door. She touched her slender fingers to my face briefly. 'Good luck.'

It gave me a charge of energy, that touch. I ran, ran, up and down the streets and stairs and in and out of garden gates. Nine-fifteen, nine-thirty, ten.

I was five minutes late and the minibus was waiting, Curtis in the driver's seat, his fingers going taptaptap on the steering wheel. The bus was empty, meaning I was being picked up first.

He wound down the window. 'How many sets?'

Not, *Did you make a sale?* but, *How many sets?*

This was the cold slap of reality and I couldn't get my words out. 'I, er, um —'

'*Weak shit. Blow-out.* Give me your kit.'

I passed it through the window to him.

He started the engine, put the bus into gear and

moved off slowly. 'Is this a holiday you're on? Think it's okay to take it easy, maybe? Come on, Ben, let's see some movement in those weak shit legs of yours.'

And I had to keep pace with the bus, trotting down the long streets, marking time as he collected the other members of the team. 'Failure,' he said. 'Weak shit.'

He forced me to run like that as far as the freeway on-ramp before he pulled over. I climbed into the back. By now I could feel pain in my chest, torn and ragged as if the air I was breathing was doing me no good at all. The others were silent. They wouldn't look at me. I couldn't blame them. I wouldn't want to draw Curtis's attention to myself if I were in their shoes.

We didn't get to bed until two in the morning. We had an attitude problem, Curtis told us. 'Learn the sales presentation,' he said. 'I want you word perfect.' And we were so tired that we faltered and stumbled, and all the while he screamed at us. I can still feel his spittle on my face, speckling my clothes. We didn't dare wipe it off.

I was up at seven the next morning, same as usual, only this time I got in first. 'Mr Curtis, I sold an almanac last night.'

He stared at me. 'I realise that, Ben. It's written here in black and white in your daily report sheet. Very good. But tell me, Ben — are you going to reach the top, are you going to be a *winner*, by selling almanacs? I mean, correct me if I'm wrong, but what I thought we were on about here is *selling encyclopaedias.*'

More spittle on my face.

'What we're going to do, Ben, is go back to this Caterina person and sell her a set of encyclopaedias, okay? She's what we call in the business a nibble — like a fish. We're going to go back there today and we're going to land this fish.'

He looked around at the others. 'You guys stay here. Spend the day perfecting your technique, while I show this blow-out how it's done.'

Twenty minutes later he was parking the minibus. 'What are you talking about, weak shit? There's no old house here.'

He was right. There was only the brick-veneer place.

Then, just as it had happened the night before, the details swam into focus in the filtered light of the morning sun, and I pointed to the stone wall and Cat's house looming behind it. 'There.'

He blinked. 'Oh. Right.'

He followed me through the side gate and up to the front door. Curtis was not wearing a tracksuit or Reeboks this time. He was looking cool and snappy in a grey double-breaster, the creases like blades, the shirt crisp and white against the solarium tan on his cruel good looks. I knocked.

'Ben!' Cat said, opening the door wide.

Then she smiled at Curtis, and it was a smile to dazzle the world. My heart sank.

'Come in, both of you.'

The room from the night before. She'd been writing letters, playing the violin. Sunlight poured through the bay window. There was a steeple in the distance, a sense of peace. Burglar alarms, police helicopters, toxins in the air, TV sets blaring inanely — it was as if those things had never existed in the world.

Just then Mr Dysart barged across the room, tugging on his white gloves. I winked at Cat. 'Still in a hurry.'

She grinned. 'He sure is.'

Curtis frowned suspiciously at us. He thought we were making fun of him. To deflect him. Cat turned on another of her dazzling smiles.

It made Curtis glow. I could see the wheels turning in his head. I could sense the heat and greed in him. I could quite happily have strangled him at that point.

He turned to face me. 'Ben, Miss Caterina and I have business to discuss. I noticed that you had several miscalls last night. I want you to go back over your beat, concentrating on those addresses where no one was at home.'

I didn't want to leave Cat there alone with Curtis. I didn't want to picture his wet lips, his confidence, her slight body bending away from him.

Or toward him. What did she want? There was a look almost like anticipation on her face.

I looked away, burning, burning, toward the window, wishing him dead.

Then Cat said — or maybe her low, throaty voice

simply appeared in my head — 'It can be done, Ben. No one would know.'

A chill crept through me. All my nerve endings were concentrated on the window seat. I could smell death. It was an old house. Plenty of people must have died there over the years. Mr Dysart and all those who came before him and all those who came after him. But why was I feeling it now? Why the window seat?

I blinked awake.

'Okay, Ben?' Curtis was saying. 'Off you go.' He winked, punched my arm playfully. 'Show 'em, Ben. I know you can do it.'

I let myself out. Curtis was murmuring to Cat even before I'd left the room. And I could hear her laughing at the things he was saying, a gurgle of pure delight that scoured me like acid.

A few nights later, Suzie, from one of the other teams, made a sale. A genuine sale, not Curtis bullshit aimed at firing up the rest of us. Curtis's reaction? He gave her a brief hug and a kiss, said well done, and went off into daydream land again. Meeting Cat had changed him. No more spitting anger, no more punches, no more sliding among us when he was least expected or wanted. He wasn't contented, exactly, or nicer. Obsessed and distracted are the words I'd use. He looked thinner, hungrier, a sharkish glint on his front teeth. He'd disappear during the day and be late picking us up at night. He also gave us a whole new bunch of suburbs to cover, kilometres away from the street where Cat lived, and that brought an ache to my heart. I'm not stupid. I could put two and two together.

My concentration began to slip. My spirit flagged. I felt alone and unwanted and far from home. The others were all competing like crazy, encouraged by Suzie's example, and reports were coming in of other sales. Not that anyone was getting paid anything — Suzie herself told me that Colman International pocketed her commission to cover her training and accommodation. The thing is, she smiled as she said it, as if that was perfectly okay with her.

In the end I couldn't bear it. We were supposed to hang around being enthusiastic during the day, but I couldn't be enthusiastic when my head was full of Cat, of doubts and questions. I figured that if I could get the answers I wanted, I'd be the most enthusiastic kid on the block, and if I didn't, I'd pack up and go home.

So I hitchhiked to the shopping centre and withdrew fifty dollars from the hole in the wall. It was money my father had given me before I left home. The old man hadn't wanted me to take the job. 'It sounds suss to me, son,' he'd said, and he'd given me five hundred bucks 'safety net' money, instructing me not to tell Colman International that I had it. I'd been a smartarse about it, telling him I wouldn't need it. 'I'll be rolling home in a Porsche for Christmas, dead set,' I told him.

He gave me his tired smile and said he hoped so, but meanwhile take the money anyway, just in case.

Good old Dad. I crammed the fifty bucks into my pocket and five minutes later I was giving Cat's address to a taxi driver.

Something odd happened. It was not Cat I thought of during that taxi ride but my father. I couldn't see all of him, only his head, chest and shoulders. There was a look of longing and vulnerability on his face. Now, my old man is a rock. I'd never seen a look like that on his face. It was as if he wanted me to come home.

The taxi drew up outside the brick-veneer house and I paid the driver twenty bucks. I saw with a sinking heart that Curtis's minibus was parked under the plane tree. I knew it. Here was my answer.

The taxi driver was filling out his log. I was just about to hire him again when the gate clanged in the ivied wall and Curtis came stamping out. He looked pinchfaced with anger and disappointment and didn't notice me there. A door slammed. A puff of exhaust, a squeal of tyres and he was gone.

Then I felt a shift in the atmosphere, as if I were being told it was okay to go in and see Cat.

She snatched the door open before I'd even lifted the lion's-head knocker. Her arms snaked around my neck, she fitted her long, slender shape against me, and I could feel her lips pulling gently on my earlobe, sending a violent charge across the surface of my skin.

Her voice in my head: 'That awful man.'

We went to her bedroom and it was the most natural thing in the world.

Later, propped on one elbow, she regarded me gravely in the curtained light, her palm resting on my chest. She was sad-sweet about something. 'Your father,' she said, and I knew exactly what it was about.

I nodded. 'He's been in a road smash. He wants me to come home.'

'Yes.'

Her palm on my skin, filling me with love.

Twenty bucks back to the caravan park. 'Blow-out.' Curtis said, his old self again. 'Where were you? Head office has been on the line. Your *mother* has been calling them.' He said it with a twist of distaste in his voice, as if no one had mothers anymore. 'Weak shit. Have you been writing sob letters home or something? You've got an attitude problem, pal.'

He was the one with the attitude problem. I hit him with an old favourite, *Up your nose with a rubber hose*, and packed my bag.

'Blow-out.'

'I'll be back, Curtis.' No more *Mister* Curtis for me.

'Don't hurry.'

Dad's five hundred dollars bought me a return ticket on Ansett with plenty to spare. I found him with one leg in plaster, nurses buzzing around him, flowers and grapes blooming beside his hospital bed. Mum was there with the twins, who were attacking his plastered shin with textas, scrawling autographs, insults, noughts and crosses.

It was good to see them. I'd come from the arms of one kind of love into the arms of another, and there were tears in my eyes. I grabbed my father's hand. 'Just as well he sideswiped you, Dad, and didn't collect you head-on.'

His smile faltered. 'How did you know that? No one's sure what happened.'

Whoops, almost caught out! To cover up I said, 'Next time, drive a Volvo, Pops.' It was an old joke between us. Dad liked to heap scorn on Volvo owners.

He seemed to mend rapidly and came home a few days later. Soon I wasn't needed and, sensing my itchy feet one morning, my father said, 'No need to hang around, son. I'll be fine. Go back to your job.'

So I returned to Sydney again, burning to see Cat, burning to put an encyclopaedia into every home in Australia. Enthusiasm? Man, I invented it.

I found a few changes. Kids come and kids go, in the encyclopaedia game. I felt as if I were an old hand among the new faces. We had a new set of managers, too, and new target areas mapped out. There was no sign of Curtis. He simply quit one day, that's all anyone knew or cared about Curtis.

And we were busy, busy, busy, too busy for me to see Cat for a while. The new managers were clones of

Curtis, forever slapping us around and shouting abuse. I didn't care. After Curtis, nothing scared me. I made two sales in my first week back. Colman pocketed most of it, recouping the cost of my training, food and lodging, but I didn't mind — I was on a roll. A few weeks like that and I'd be taking Cat for a spin in my Porsche.

No I wouldn't. Who was I kidding? What a nerd. A Porsche wasn't going to impress her.

That led me to thinking about what it was about me that *did* impress her. The old who-am-I question, and it hit me pretty hard. What was I to Cat? Without her, what was I to myself?

Colman International didn't sell on Monday nights. It's not a good selling night. People don't feel anxious about their kids' education until the end of the week, and they've usually blown their pay cheques by Monday anyway, taking the kids to Pizza Hut, or betting on slow racehorses — or for all I know buying vacuum cleaners from door-to-door salesmen.

So I walked to the shopping centre just off the freeway exit ramp on the first available Monday evening, splashed out fifteen bucks on a dozen red roses, and took a taxi to Cat's house.

It struck me every time I went there that it was a difficult place to find. An average suburban street that runs into other streets just like it, except this one seemed to have a hidden heart to it, a space you'd miss if you blinked or didn't know where and how to look.

With all the strong sunlight striking off glass and chrome and duco that day, I almost walked right past the wall without seeing it.

And for the first time I noticed how ordinary the house really was. Peeling paint, dead shrubs, cracked putty in the window frames. It wasn't such a big place, either. I thought, *What's happening here, Ben? A dose of reality at last?*

And Cat wasn't there. She didn't answer my knocking. The curtains were drawn over every window. There was only one tiny gap where the window seat was, and all I could see was bare floorboards.

I found a key behind a loose brick at the front of the house. My footsteps rang out like Nazi jackboots in the empty hallway — through the house, past the paintings, the staircase, into the room where Cat had first shown me who I was. Floorboards like a vast, dry plain. A desert of a room.

Except for that window seat.

Come with me. One step at a time across the booming floor.

Lift the lid with me.

And recoil from the horror.

I don't know how Curtis died, or how he was killed, only that his death must have been a journey through hell. His teeth were bared in a death grimace, his eyes were open, riveted, as though he could see death coming. He saw her, he saw the deathdealer.

In the end I left him in that stale, dry place. I imagined his decomposition, his gases expanding, his fluids pooling inside him. His face was a death mask, shrinking, mummifying, and in the end I shut the lid on it.

I'm telling it how it happened. I found myself defending the company for a while after I quit. I couldn't go past a house that had nappies on the line without wanting to go in and sell, sell, sell. I couldn't get used to passengers sitting so quiet and still in trains and buses — why weren't they being enthusiastic?

I've never been able to find the house again, though I used to go back to the street, hoping I'd find everything unchanged, hoping that time had been out of joint the day I found Cat gone and Curtis in his vault. It's taken me a while to realise that Curtis must have been unknown and unloved in the world, for I'm the only one who remembers him, who knows that he existed in the first place. But if *he* didn't exist, did Cat? Did I wish her into existence because I was in need of love, just as Curtis died because I'd wished him dead?

There's only one thing I know for sure: these days I hear and see exactly what's in front of me, nothing more — apart from a faint memory trace sometimes, of a soft hand resting on my chest, where my heart is.

THE ISLE OF SIGHS

She had come to a house at the end of the world — or so it seemed. Adrienne could sense the house behind her. She turned and made an effort to examine it carefully, fighting down the panic she felt, telling herself to look at the evidence the way a scientist would. Just as there was no room for emotion when she dissected frogs in the biology lab, there was no room for emotion now. It was only an old holiday house, the sort of place you and your friends could have fun in for a few days, now that the exams were over.

The evidence. Two storeys and an attic. Ivy-covered walls of local sandstone. Steeply pitched tile roof. Two tall, stiff, slender chimneys, poking like warning fingers into the sky. See? She was doing it again, bringing feelings and imagination into it. Start again:

two tall, stiff, slender chimneys like . . . chimneys. Wooden doors, window frames and shutters, weathered by sun and storms to the colour of ancient mud. Careful — don't get too fanciful. The windows in the morning sun glinting like icicles on a wintry plain.

It was no good, Adrienne couldn't help it. There was nothing neutral about Benbow Lodge. You could not look upon it with the cool gaze of reason.

She shifted her eyes. The Lodge was on a headland, screened from the coast road by a curving avenue of massive pines. She liked the grounds: weeping willows, umbrella trees, liquidambars, sundials, mossy birdbaths and cherubs carved from white stone. A barn and a couple of cobwebby sheds lay deep in the pine trees.

And the maze. It was small, tight, intricate, the trimmed-hedge walls twice her height. Adrienne went in there with the gang soon after they arrived yesterday afternoon, and they circled the tower in the centre futilely for an hour before finding the way out.

That tower. It was thirty metres high, a spindly looking thing constructed of bamboo and small trimmed branches lashed together with twine. The tower had been a joke to them all until Rick told them about the Willow Man sacrifices in ages past, about victims bound and set alight in towers like this one.

She set out across the manicured lawn and stopped at the clifftop, where the grass became a ragged fringe. Far beneath her were shoreline rocks, pitted and channelled by centuries of heaving winds and seas. Farther out was the Isle of Sighs, a smudge in the black waters like something tossed aside and forgotten. A seagull, a distant tanker. Otherwise there was only the sea and the sky.

Adrienne turned her back to the house again and sat on the grass, looking out to sea, her legs dangling over the clifftop. She didn't know what to make of Rick. He was the odd one out, just as she was. Six kids: two couples and two left over. Adrienne wondered if the couples had planned it that way. She was a well-known swot, so was Rick, and Adrienne was betting the others were matchmaking, trying to get her together with Rick now that the exams were over.

Well, she didn't know how to go about it, and she didn't think Rick did either, and even if she did want to sneak into his room one night, or he into hers, what kind of privacy could they expect? The others — Stef 'n' Kate, Tim 'n' Tina — would be full of smirks and knowing looks at breakfast the next morning.

Assuming she wanted to go to bed with someone, would it be Rick? One, he was a know-all. Two, he had a high-pitched laugh, the kind that was a turnoff, not infectious. Three, he didn't seem to notice that his glasses sat crookedly on his nose. She itched to straighten them sometimes. Four, he was always plunged into a deep depression, joking with a black edge about death, fate, purpose, the meaning of things.

At least that was more interesting than the blonde, suntanned, empty wholesomeness of Tim 'n' Tina and Stef 'n' Kate, but if anyone thought Adrienne was put on this earth to save Rick from himself, they had another think coming.

She looked out upon the glassy sea. Seven a.m. The others wouldn't be up for hours yet. Rick wasn't the type to get up early. Tim 'n' Tina, Stef 'n' Kate? Glorious freedom for a change. No parents snooping around. Adrienne tried to imagine them in the throes of passion. She tried to imagine it of herself, with . . . who?

The Isle of Sighs. It was a small, irregular hump in the water, one tiny sandy beach, with mangroves and ti-trees struggling over the hump. Adrienne wished she'd brought binoculars with her. Apparently there were ruins on the island, and an acre of gravestones. She pictured them in her mind, silent, tilted, worn, like stumpy teeth in the grass.

She was really putting science and reason behind her now. It felt good. She liked knowing that she had an imagination, after a year of sober study. A sensation close to dread pricked the skin on her forearms, and she gave herself up to it.

The Isle of Sighs, the saddest place on earth. It was where the convicts had gone to die, pickpockets, vagrants and thieves who had sickened in the colony a hundred and sixty years ago and been kept apart from the healthy prisoners. Some of them escaped, slipping through the sharks to the rocky shore beneath her. Some murdered settlers in their beds, some were hunted down on horseback, and some hid and were never seen again.

She hadn't heard anyone leave the lodge but at that moment hands began to press against her back, pushing teasingly. 'Stop it,' she said, half frowning, half laughing.

But then the push became a hard, insistent shove. Adrienne felt herself sliding toward the cliff's edge. She put her hands out, tore uselessly at the grass. Pebbles scraped her bare legs. The empty air between the clifftop and the rocky beach opened up before her, the hands continued to push, push, and Adrienne's last word on this earth was pitched on the far side of terror. *'No!'*

The pushing stopped. She felt the hands release her. She scrambled back to safety, anger taking the place of fear. She turned, snarling, her heart hammering, ready to lash out.

Nothing.

There was no one behind her, no one even remotely near her.

There was only the empty lawn, the quiet stone house. Let science and reason explain *that*, Adrienne thought, when her heart and her breathing were calmer.

Tim 'n' Tina surfaced first. Adrienne watched them covertly from an armchair in a bay window of the vast downstairs room, a book in her lap, wings of her black hair screening her eyes. Tim 'n' Tina were like Siamese twins, permanently joined. She saw them descend the wooden stairs entwined together, pour milk over bowls of muesli without releasing one another, sit thigh to thigh and head to head on a bench at the long table in the centre of the room. Even as she watched, one bare foot hooked against another. They wore identical shorts and T-shirts. They had identical heads — tousled sandy hair, heavy eyelids, faces a little swollen with sleep and passion.

Adrienne felt a tug in her heart, a complicated emotion of envy and disdain. She concentrated on her book. Now and then, soft murmurs and low, throaty laughter reached her across the room. She tried to ignore it.

Then Rick appeared. He was tidy and cheerful, and had sleek comb marks in his wet hair. 'Hey, Addie,' he said, sitting opposite her with a plate of raisin toast. 'Want some?'

She thought, why not? and put down her book. The toast was dripping with honey. 'You're looking cheerful this morning. Where's your doom and gloom about the world?'

'Best sleep I ever had,' Rick said. 'Exams over, freedom, fresh air, no one hassling me, no shouting matches keeping me awake all night.'

Adrienne supposed that he meant his parents. He'd

never given her the slightest glimpse of life at home before. She said, 'The sleep of the innocent?'

'Exactly. How about you, bed comfortable?'

She shrugged. This conversation was getting onto the subject of sleep and beds already. 'Fine.'

They munched in silence, Rick grinning happily at her. When he did that, kindness wrinkles showed at the edges of his eyes. She smiled back.

He pounced. *'Got you!* A smile, an actual smile.'

'You can talk.'

Rick crammed more toast into his mouth. There was honey on his chin and he was not so appealing now. He said, his mouth full, 'Today is the first day of the rest of my life.'

'That's a tired old saying,' Adrienne said, picking up her book again. 'Wipe your chin, Sunshine.'

He did, unabashed, grinning at her. She folded her long legs into the deepness of the armchair and began to read.

The scream came from somewhere in the top part of the house. Adrienne was reminded of her own scream — all hope gone — and felt her skin creep. She jerked out of her chair.

Pounding feet above. Then Kate appeared at the head of the staircase. She wore a scarlet kimono tied at the waist, and nothing on her feet. Her short plump legs looked white, awkward and panicky on the steps, as if they were betraying her just when she needed speed. She reached the bottom and sped toward the front door, the soles of her feet slapping the slate tiles, her hair flying. She reached the lawn and didn't stop.

'Too cool,' Rick said, watching her through the bay window.

Tim 'n' Tina had scarcely looked up.

Adrienne threw down her book. 'Any of you ever heard of compassion?'

She found Kate curled into a corner of a wooden bench near the maze, face hidden, clasping her knees, rocking endlessly. Adrienne sat next to her. After a moment, she reached out her hand and touched Kate's shoulder. Kate sprang open, electric with fear and hate. Her face was distorted, tear-streaked, searching for the danger. Both of her hands flailed at Adrienne's face.

Adrienne jerked back. 'Katie, it's me.'

Kate stiffened, stared at her, and curled into a ball again. She began to rock. Her voice came in a muffle: 'It's not him.'

Adrienne reached out and stroked the tangled hair. 'Stefan?'

Kate looked up. 'It's not him.'

Adrienne felt her anger rising. 'What did he do to you?'

Kate shook her head. 'Nothing like that. It was beautiful, and then I woke up and something about him was different. It's not him.'

'Did he say something to hurt you?'

Kate thrashed about in frustration. 'You don't understand. I can't explain . . . it looks like Stef, sounds like him, the same chip in his front tooth, but *it's not him*, it's not Stef. His eyes. His mood. He's different, there's nothing there.'

Adrienne slid her arms around Kate, feeling pity for her. Love dies, passion cools, it was something that happened between people. Stefan had probably been full of ardour for Kate last night, but now, in the cold light of day, he no longer wanted her. The face and the body can't lie about things like that. Adrienne rocked Kate gently, stroking her, saying, 'It's all right, it's all right.'

'What will I do?'

Adrienne didn't know. She said nothing. Time passed and they rocked together and both of them drew comfort from it.

A soft whine broke their trance. Adrienne became aware of a warm weight pressing on her knee, a panting gulp, a lolling tongue. She laughed. 'Kate, look.'

The dog seemed to be offering reassurance. It was an old labrador, happy with life, giving and expecting love. His tail beat softly on the ground.

Kate's face lit up. She climbed down from the bench and hugged the dog. Adrienne fondled his ears. There was a tag on his collar. 'His name is Lincoln.'

'He must belong to one of the farms.'

They got up and walked back to the house. Lincoln, apparently satisfied that he'd cured their unhappiness, wandered nose down past the maze and back into the trees.

The next part was going to be difficult. Stefan was probably up by now, seated with the others at the long table. We're stuck with each other for a whole week, Adrienne thought, so we can hardly avoid him. But that doesn't mean we have to talk to him or spend time in his company.

He was there, just as she'd feared. He looked up as they came through the door, gazed at them calmly for a moment, and returned to the book propped open before him on the sugar bowl. Stifling a sob, Kate ran past him to the stairs and out of sight.

Adrienne returned to the armchair in the bay window. She was alone in the big room with Stefan. Tim 'n' Tina had left their plates on the table; Rick's half-consumed raisin toast sat on the floor next to the standard lamp. Adrienne didn't know where they were, nor did she care. She was living among people who were careless and self-absorbed, and her only welcome thought on this first day of a long week was the knowledge that she had a bag full of novels in her room upstairs.

She opened her book and began to read. Soon she had entered a world of great promise and satisfaction. The only sound was the regular scrape of paper as she turned the pages, but she didn't even hear that. If Tim, Tina, Stefan or Kate moved above or around her, she didn't notice them. The clock ticked in the hallway.

The blood pumped silently, regularly, through her veins.

It was a movement so slight that she almost failed to register it. Had air eddied at the curtain's edge? She looked across at the armchair where Rick had been sitting. It was empty. She looked beyond it at the big room. There was no one seated at the table. She returned to her book.

This time she sensed a face and a body, limbs settling in Rick's chair. She looked directly at the chair and saw nothing. Looked at it glancingly, from the corner of her eyes, and saw a figure seated there.

She froze. She felt cold, her heart hesitating, dread creeping through her. It can't be there and not there, she told herself. She faced the other chair, full on, staring hard at it. Definitely empty.

Don't show fear, don't fall apart, try a cool, scientific, edge-of-the-eye examination of this phenomenon.

Adrienne bent her head to the book in her lap, kept it steady, and swivelled her eyes a little.

The man was indistinct, like smoke, like the trace of a man, but she recognised the emotions in his face. It was a ravaged, hollow-cheeked face so drawn and old and tired that nothing on this earth could console it.

Adrienne felt herself floating, as though he were drawing her soul's essence into himself.

She blinked and looked up and she was alone in the big room.

I can't bear this, she thought, wrapping both arms about herself and hurrying out of the house to where the air smelt of ordinary things and the sun would warm her bones.

Rick was throwing a frisbee in a low, slicing arc across the lawn. Lincoln, new life in his old frame, backed up, facing it, ducking and weaving as he tried to anticipate its fall. He locked into position suddenly, leapt, and snatched the frisbee from the sky. Rick cheered. Lincoln trotted across the grass, the frisbee clamped wetly in his jaws. Adrienne thought that she had never seen anything so welcome and harmless as the old dog and the boy she'd known through high school. She ran down the slope to join them.

Lincoln endured the game for another two minutes then wandered off again. He was a dog with a life full of missions. Adrienne and Rick followed him, talking idly. 'It's true, you know,' Rick said.

'What is?'

'There's beauty in simple things.'

He could have been reading her thoughts. 'Yes.' she said.

'I've been so locked in gloom and doom that I've forgotten how to see the world.'

In reply, Adrienne linked her arm in his. She felt him tense, then relax, and they walked on, their hips bumping, falling into an effortless rhythm as if they'd spent all of their lives walking as lovers do.

'It was just the exams getting you down,' Adrienne said.

'No, I'm gloomy by nature. But now that I recognise it . . .' He didn't go on.

Adrienne squeezed his arm encouragingly. After a while she said, 'Stefan and Kate had a falling out.'

'All better now, though.'

She stopped, unhooking her arm from his. 'What do you mean?'

'While you were reading I was up in the attic looking through all the junk, and I overheard them making up.'

Adrienne sighed. She took his arm again. 'Well, it's nothing to do with us.'

They came to a clearing and stopped. Lincoln was rolling on his back in the dirt, grunting with satisfaction. They stood and watched.

'Rick,' Adrienne said slowly, wondering how to phrase it, 'have you noticed anything odd since you've been here?'

'Not really. Why?'

'It just seems spooky to me, somehow.'

Rick thought about it. 'Can't say that I've noticed. Except . . .'

Her grip tightened. 'What?'

'Stefan was a bit weird this morning. I was ringing my mother —' Rick shifted his shoulders, embarrassed, '— she likes to know I'm okay, you know. So I'm ringing home and suddenly Stefan is there, watching me. *That* was creepy. It was as if he'd never seen anyone use a telephone before.'

Adrienne didn't know what to make of that. Until she saw the evidence, she couldn't comment. She turned with Rick and they walked slowly back to the house.

She realised that she hadn't eaten for fifteen hours. 'Time for lunch.'

'A picnic,' Rick said, pushing his glasses up his nose.

Adrienne watched, fascinated, as he did it. The frame was definitely crooked. She reached up, plucked the glasses off his face, and sighted along each arm. One was twisted at the hinge. 'Anyone would think you wore your glasses to bed.'

'I tend to sit on them,' Rick said.

Adrienne straightened the bent arm, hooked the glasses onto his face again. 'Perfect.'

Rick stared at her, his jaw dropping open in amazement, as if he were seeing her for the first time. 'You mean that's what you really look like? Radical. To think of all the time I've wasted lusting after other women.'

She punched him. 'Don't blow it, Sunshine.' Then she hooked her arm in his. 'A picnic on the beach?'

Adrienne liked feeling his skinny flank against her. She wanted the others to notice and comment this time. She wanted them to tease her a little.

But by the time they reached the house there had been another shift in the atmosphere. Kate, Stefan and Tina were sitting shoulder to shoulder on a bench at the long table, perfectly groomed, utterly still and silent. The irritating teenage blankness was gone from their faces, replaced by the pleasant, watchful expressions of people who have the patience of the centuries. They looked up mildly as she passed through the door with Rick. 'Hello, Adrienne, hello, Rick,' they said, and there was no curiosity, no smirking, to see her arm in arm with Rick, only acceptance, all three pairs of eyes steady and unblinking, a little yellow in the dim light of the house.

Tim was sitting in the armchair in the bay window, as far apart from the others as he could get. Evidently they had ganged up on him about something. He was slumped in the chair, looking desolately through the window to the sloping lawn and the Isle of Sighs in the bay.

Adrienne murmured to Kate, 'Feeling better?'

Kate replied immediately, her voice ringing clear and emotionless: 'Oh yes, thank you, Adrienne. Thank you for asking.'

Adrienne felt a chill in her heart: all the emotion seemed to have drained from Kate. Rick frowned. He'd also noticed the mood shift. 'We thought we'd go for a picnic.'

At once the three swung their legs over the bench

and spoke in unison: 'What a good idea. I shall cut the sandwiches. I shall make a flask of tea. I shall prepare a basket.' And they walked in single file to the kitchen.

'Too weird,' Rick said. 'Are they having a go at us?'

'Who knows? You fetch some blankets from upstairs. I'll see if Tim wants to come.'

Tim still hadn't showered or changed his clothes. His hair was uncombed, his face creased and puffy with sleep. He didn't look up until Adrienne blocked his view through the window.

'Leave me alone.'

'We're going on a picnic. Want to come?'

'Count me out.'

'Come on, Timbo. It's a beautiful day. You don't want to be stuck inside this creepy house. Don't you want to be with Tina?'

'Yeah, right, with a robot.'

She sat on the arm of his chair. 'Did you and Tina have a fight?'

'It's as if someone turned a switch. She was all right this morning, then we went back to bed —' he blushed '— you know, and I woke up and she was all cold and distant, as if I'm a bad smell.'

Adrienne touched his arm. 'We've all had a hard year. Exams, now the big wait for the results. Give her time to unwind.'

He didn't reply. Adrienne stood to go. Tim was irritating her. They all were, except Rick. Self-involved, self-pitying, ungenerous, she could go on and on. They expected *her* to be consumed with *their* thoughts, feelings and relationships, as if she had none of these herself. It wouldn't hurt them to show some interest in her for a change.

'We're going now,' she said. 'You suit yourself.'

He stayed. Adrienne, Rick and the others filed out of the house and across the lawn to the clifftop. A switchback path led down to the tiny beach, crumbling in places as it cut back and forth across the face of the cliff. At the bottom they clambered over the rockfall to the gritty sand beyond, searching for dry, flat areas among the kelp. Gulls slipped down the air currents above them. The sea lapped at the shoreline, as black and sluggish as oil or blood.

Adrienne spread a blanket on the sand and shared out the sandwiches. Rick collapsed beside her. To her considerable relief, Stefan, Kate and Tina chose to position themselves several metres away, so that only their backs were visible as they stared toward the bleak island in the bay.

Now that she was sitting at sea level, Adrienne had a clear sense of the shape of the Isle of Sighs. There were three humps at the centre, outlined hazily by trees. And the island didn't seem to be rooted in the water; it appeared to hover above the surface. Something to do with the light at the horizon, Adrienne guessed, remembering a passage in a science textbook.

But mostly she was interested in the way pleasure waves ran through her when Rick fitted his long shape against her, his chin on her scalp, his arm around her waist. She could feel his heartbeat, hear his steady breathing, feel the warmth of him. All this was new to her and new to him — and Tina, Kate and Stefan didn't seem to know or care a damn.

She looked across at them. They were sitting in a row, straightbacked, looking at the heavy waters of the bay. Well, who cares about them? she thought.

Then someone shouted 'Oi!', and pebbles pattered the sand. She looked up. It was Tim, guiding Lincoln along the path by his collar. Lincoln's tongue was lolling happily, his tail beating Tim's legs. Poor Tim, looking for love where he could find it.

Another shower of pebbles hit the beach. 'Careful,' Rick called.

At the final stretch of the path. Lincoln strained forward and Tim let him go. Adrienne watched Lincoln's clumsy, eager, misshapen old body with affection. She whistled to him, holding up a sandwich, and saw him plunge onto the beach and set out across the sand toward her.

And she saw him freeze. She saw his legs and body stiffen in a half crouch, hairs springing up along his spine. He bared his teeth and snarled, quietly at first, then with increasing ferocity.

He wouldn't stop growling, even as Tim caught up

with him and put a steadying hand on his neck. Adrienne got up to help, wary until she realised that Lincoln was locked on Stefan, Tina and Kate, who continued to gaze out at the Isle of Sighs.

A cloud took away the sunlight.

Kate turned first, then Tina, then Stefan, perfectly synchronised, turning their incurious yellow eyes upon the barking dog.

The change in Lincoln was immediate. He swallowed a snarl and backed away, his belly scraping the sand, his tail between his legs, yipping in fear. Adrienne touched his spine in reassurance. Great shudders were passing through him. Then Lincoln cried out a final time and turned and scrabbled up through the loops of the path to the clifftop above.

Tim scowled at the three figures at the sea's edge, now facing the island again. He called the words of an old song over the sand, directing pain and anger at Tina's back: 'You're as cold as ice . . .'

For all Adrienne knew, the afternoon and the evening dragged, the tension unbearable, but she didn't notice, didn't care. Let the others sort themselves out — she spent the time making up for all the experiences she'd sacrificed during the year to that great god, Exams. She wanted to stare at Rick through the hours and days and years. He made her laugh. She made him laugh. Whenever there was no part of him touching her, she felt that a part of her was missing. There were new sensations in her belly and in her heart, and she marvelled at them. She hoped that time might stop still.

For dinner Rick phoned a pizza shop in the nearest town. Thirty minutes later, a pink van delivered three mediums with the lot, no anchovies, no pineapple. She was hungry, Rick was hungry. Tim sat alone in the bay window, picking at his food. Stefan, Kate and Tina? They sat politely in a row at the long table, chewing in unison, four slices each, exactly as though they were machines in need of fuel. They seemed to get no enjoyment out of it. Adrienne didn't care. It was nothing to do with her.

At ten o'clock she climbed the stairs, Rick at her side. By now they knew which step was the creaking one and avoided it together, giggling a little, feeling light-headed and inane and in love.

By an unspoken decision they parted at the head of the stairs. There was time enough tomorrow night or the next for the thing they both wanted. Adrienne went to her room and Rick to his. A short time later, she heard Tim go to his room. She fell asleep then. Stefan and the girls could stay up all night for all she cared.

She was woken by a staircreak. Two o'clock. Someone going down for a glass of water, she thought. She felt thirsty, too, and blamed the salty pizza. Her curtains were open. Cloudy moonlight patterned the walls and the ceiling, showing yellow in the wardrobe mirror. Adrienne tried to drift into sleep again. She turned onto her side, hugging a pillow to her stomach. Rick would be like this in her arms.

Two-fifteen. She got up, crossed to the window. The bay in the moonlight was clearly defined. Spirits in a graveyard would want to walk on a night as sharp as this.

Adrienne shivered, let herself into the corridor, went step by step to the pool of blackness in the hall below. She felt her way to the kitchen. Her hand patted the wall, searching for the light switch.

The man-shape was etched against the window. She screamed.

'Adrienne,' the man said.

She found the switch. Light flooded the kitchen. 'Tim! You scared me half to death. What are you doing here in the dark?'

Tim stood there stiffly. 'It was not my wish to startle you, Adrienne.'

'Couldn't you sleep? Are you still upset about Tina?'

His voice was clear, accentless, empty of feeling as if he were the dry husk of a man. 'I am well, thank you, Adrienne. It was kind of you to ask. Good night, Adrienne.'

He went by her into the darkness of the house. Adrienne told herself not to be silly, that warm blood pulsed in Tim and nothing dead ever walked the night.

But fear gripped her. The night with its darkness,

and her bed empty and cold, were unendurable. She heard her bare feet on the slate, on the stairs, on the creaking step. She let them lead her along the hall above, past the closed doors of the people who had once been her friends.

Rick had chosen a room at the end. The handle turned easily, the door soundless on its hinges. Adrienne found him waiting for her at the window, looking out at the bay, at the Isle of Sighs black on the silver water like a shape snipped from a sheet of tin. He turned. His eyes in the yellow light were flickerless and Adrienne wanted to run from them and she wanted to drown herself in them.

THE DIFFERENCE TO ME

Unrequited love drove the young man from his home and circle of friends to a rented room in a house in one of those unexpected streets along the bank of the river that divides the city. He gave his new address to his family. They raised their eyebrows as if to say, *That slum?*, so he found himself pointing out that there was a wonderful park just five minutes walk away.

A freeway made a snarling loop less than half a kilometre from the house, and there was a brewery in the next street, but the young man liked to claim that the noise and the smell didn't bother him. In fact, he found sleep difficult, and even though the brewery had a high chimney, it wasn't high enough, and the smell lingered. From a vantage point next to the blackberry-choked backyard fence above the river he could hear the big trucks change gear and see the black tip of the chimney.

And the people with whom he shared the house told him to watch where he walked, because snakes sometimes slid up from the river, into the garden.

In the old streets nearby, tiny factories manufactured boots and shoes, chipboard bookcases and racks and racks of cheap dresses. The bus he took to the university crawled along a road choked at all hours of the day and night with cars. Commuters hated taking this route, there were too many traffic lights, but they had no choice. They crawled along. The air was offensive. Everything gave the young man a headache.

But now and then the wind blew it all away, or he thought there might be signs of an improvement in his outlook. Perhaps the girl in the front room and the couple in the side room would go away for the weekend and he would have the house to himself. He had his books and his piano and the TV set. There were chairs under the loquat tree in the back garden. The others said feel free to borrow their books, and, when they were away and the house was quiet, he liked to stand in their rooms and listen and think and sniff the air. But then he would be racked with enormous yawns and the days would seem endless.

One day the young man blurted out his loneliness and heartache to a friend and she said, 'Keep busy, keep fit.' That reminded him of the park: he would have to go there sooner or later. He bought an expensive pair of running shoes and, twice a day, between lectures and tutorials, he set out for a long walk. He walked past shop windows to see his feet flashing, see the dazzling red stripes flashing as he went silently by in his chunky, prowling running shoes. *Snicker hush* was the sound they made on the roadway, and only he could hear it.

He liked to vary his route. He could enter the park by way of the footbridge at the bottom, or the street at the top, or the bicycle path that traced the river bank. He thought that he would never see a tree as lovely as a weeping willow. Absurd phrases like this went through his head.

Now and then men from the council would come in to slash and paint and clean, but mostly the grass grew long, rotting tree-trunks lay across the paths, branches cracked and fell in the distance, and the swings squeaked for lack of oil. The young man preferred it like that. It was a large, untidy park, and almost no one used it.

After a few days he began to notice that a man with a limp, and accompanied by a small female dog, also set out at ten o'clock and three o'clock every day. An unreasoning resentment filled him. He didn't want to change his times, so he decided to change his route.

For the next few weeks he entered the park only by the bicycle path, then cut across the small sunlit hollow which he liked to think of as a meadow, and left near the freeway at the top. He couldn't avoid the man and his dog by taking this route, but at least he didn't have to meet them face to face. Instead, he came upon them from behind. He would pass the fellow, pass the competent little dog, his striding walk saying that he had things to do, places to go. And as he went by he'd hear breathing, full of pain and effort, and the scrabbling sounds of a little snout in the long grass.

That was the early period. The days grew wintry and the young man wrapped himself in his thoughts. Bit by bit, however, he realised that he was opening up to the world around him — who owned what car, which house the pigeons flew to every evening, the important days in the Greek religious calendar. Everyone was mad about football.

Sometimes, when he was on his way to the bank or the laundromat, the young man saw the dog man walking without his dog. He was a man who walked and walked, criss-crossing the little suburb, leaning all of his weight onto one leg. The young man hoped that the dog man had someone to talk to, and was pleased when he saw him go into a corner pub one day.

Then a week later he saw the man leave a corner shop with a meat pie. 'Hello,' he said, before he could stop himself.

The dog man's face looked baffled and uncontrolled; he had trouble with his pie. The young man saw loose muscles in the man's face, and muscles that would never work again, and thought: *Poor guy, he's had a stroke.* The realisation came quickly, and he didn't pause as he strode by, but a second or two later he heard a muffled human sound behind him that might have been a greeting in response.

Now that this had happened, now that he had initiated something for a change and not waited for something to happen, the young man felt that he could cross the park in any direction he chose. Winter became spring and the locals rediscovered the park. Kids did stunts on their rollerblades. Youths racketed out of nowhere on trail bikes. On Friday afternoons distressed fat boys and skinny asthmatic boys lurched past him, their white legs a burden to them, and somewhere up ahead there would be a teacher waiting with a stopwatch. Now and then he saw men standing darkly in the clearings to the side of the rough tracks in the deepest reaches of the park. He had heard of men like these, and averted his eyes. *Snakes in the grass*, he thought.

Every day he saw the man with the limp, stepping forward with his good leg and giving a hitch and lean as he dragged his unproductive leg after him. Step and drag, step and drag, day after day. There might have been a soft moan or a wheeze or a creaking sound with every step.

The little black dog, quivering with nerves and curiosity, would sniff around old logs and under bushes. She handled long grass by making short, belly-flopping flights, her legs and tail stretched out as though to help her float above it. If she got lost in the grass she jumped up repeatedly to see where she was going, her tongue out and a mad, exultant look on her face. She'd return to the man every few minutes to explore a scent around his persevering feet, to see that he was all right. Then she had to be off again.

In this fashion the man and his dog made their way across the park at ten o'clock and three o'clock every day. The young man would remove his right hand from his pocket, raise it, and say hello as he went by.

It was quite likely that the fellow had no one but the dog in his life. During the long hours of his day he probably spoke to no one, and that was why his eyes seemed so cloaked and private. The man didn't seem to look at anything when he walked through the park. Certainly he was slow to respond when the young man greeted him. For all the response he made he might have been in a supermarket, where the voices of other people mean nothing. He kept his hands inside the pockets of a thin, dirty blue nylon jacket. When a cold wind blew he settled his neck inside his collar and pulled his woollen cap down over his ears. Strain showed on his face, and the young man could not take his eyes away from the step and drag of the man's feet, or the shape and unlikely colour of his poor, inadequate shoes.

One day the young man stopped on the footbridge

and waited. There was unseasonal rain in the air, collecting in small, cold, magnifying drops on his coat sleeves. Schoolboys ran by as he waited, setting up a vibration that he could feel through the bridge timbers. The day was a misery but schoolboys were sent out in it and the limping man and his little dog didn't seem to mind. The young man waited until they got closer and then he squatted, reached for the little dog with both hands and said, 'Here, girl.'

There were plenty of endearments he might have gone on to say, but the little dog lowered her belly to the broken-down boards of the bridge and with a scrape of her claws escaped from his grasp. The young man was left with the sensation of wet fur on the tips of his fingers. He felt foolish. He turned on his heels to make another grab and the little dog, watching him warily, made a short, panicky scramble to the safety of her master.

'She shy,' said the man with the limp. His disordered smile pulled at the muscles on one side of his face. 'Me,' he said, pointing at his chest. 'Only me.'

The young man stood and they smiled and nodded and edged past each other. 'Nice little dog.'

'Only me,' said the man. 'From when she was a puppy.'

After that it was easier between them. The man with the limp began to wait for him to appear. If they saw each other in the distance, the man would wave. If they met on a path or on the footbridge, the man would stop, his head and shoulders rocking and his mouth opening and closing, winding himself up for the short, difficult conversations they'd begun to have. The thing between them was close to a friendship.

One day the young man was out in his car, giving the girl from the front room a lift to the station, when he saw his friend — he didn't yet know the man's name — on the footpath, waiting at a pedestrian crossing. He tooted and waved. After a while the man recognised him and began his rocking, his face disorganised by a helpless smile. There were supermarket bags in his hands. He looked so vulnerable, so grateful, that the young man had to look away.

'Who on earth is that?' said the girl from the front room.

'I thought you might have seen him around the place,' the young man said.

The girl shrugged and yawned. She was bored; already something else outside the car had attracted her attention. A bitterness settled in the young man. Her manner reminded him of his life a year ago, of the girl who had said no to him. You can't get anywhere with them, he thought. They assume they're right, that they're the chosen, yet there's nothing in their heads at all. There was no point in talking to the girl from the front room about the dog man, but still he found himself saying:

'I feel sorry for him. He's cut off from everything: one, because he's had a stroke and can't work any more; two, because he comes from Latvia and hasn't got any family here; three, because it's hard to understand what he says, owing to his stroke and his accent. He's usually got a little dog with him. It's very loyal, won't let anyone else pat her.'

He looked across at the girl from the front room. After a while she gathered herself and said, for something to say, 'Where does he live?'

'I think he must live in a boarding house around here somewhere. He was telling me about his landlady. He hates her. "Blutty bitch," he calls her. "Blutty bitch." Apparently he's on the list for a Housing Commission flat but he hasn't heard anything yet and meanwhile she's trying to get rid of him. She doesn't like him having a dog.' He took one hand from the steering wheel and gestured with it. 'I can see this poky little room, draughty, grey blanket on the bed, damp . . .'

But they had reached the station and she was reaching for her bag. As she got out of the car, he said with a rush: 'He'd be better off in a Housing Commission flat, a place of his own, but he reckons they won't let him take a dog there, so he's in a real bind.'

Her mouth was open. The seconds ticked by. After a while she said, 'Oh well, something will work out. Thanks for the lift.'

On the way home his head was spinning with solutions.

Summer came. People grew crazy, cranky, eager to leave the city with the holidaying hordes. A year had passed and the young man was flooded with memories.

It was no good. He withdrew his savings, had his car serviced, packed a tent and plenty of paperbacks and cassettes, and set out to explore the coastline. He had a few small adventures and thought about the things in his life.

He got back on a hot, still day two weeks later. The city seemed empty. The house on the river ticked softly in the heat. The rooms within it were dim, peaceful, shadowy. The girl from the front room and the couple from the side room were still away and the young man liked to step through their doorways and imagine their lives. All their little things meant something to them — the soapstone snail on the mantelpiece, foreign stamps in a small cane basket, a furry glass with a smear of liqueur in the bottom of it. He skimmed their letters. There was a massage book under the bed in the side room. The girl in the front room had draped bright, filmy scarves over her chair, her bedside lamp, her typewriter. It was good to be home again.

In the late afternoons he put on his running shoes. He was pleased with them: they were pleasantly scuffed, ringed with salt stains from rock pools and the lapping waters of the sea. On his way to the park he passed Greek women watering their cement gardens and he smelt sawdust hanging in the doorways of workshops. He saw small boys drop what they were doing to gather and touch and wonder when an older brother parked his long, gleaming car in the street. Everything lifted the young man. He beamed as he went by, *snicker, hush.*

In this mood he crossed the footbridge into the park. The air there carried a thick smell of mown grass, making his eyes itchy, and he kicked at a worm of chopped grass left by the mowing machines. Instantly he stopped, helpless, attacked by a sneezing fit. He longed to dive into the river and wash it all away.

Feeling clogged and half blind, he climbed out of the trapped air in the hollows to a higher part of the park. It was the best time of the day and he wanted to survey the world.

His friend with the limp was standing, blurred by the low sun behind him, on the top path, close to a woman sprawled on a blanket. The young man gave a low, pleased shout and saw, as he drew nearer, a twist of happiness on the dog man's face.

He was stopped from saying or doing more because the woman on the blanket lowered her book and peered at him oddly. She glanced about her, then at the young man again. 'Were you addressing me?'

He smiled to reassure her. 'My friend,' he said, indicating the path behind her.

He reached the dog man. 'Holiday?' the man asked.

'Yes, holiday, two weeks.'

'Beach?'

'Yes, the beach.'

The man nodded. In the queer light he looked puffy and ill. There was a grey sheen of pain and perspiration behind his smile.

The young man turned away from it. The clean slopes of the park were like swells in an ocean. 'It's good to be back,' he said, then saw that the woman on the blanket was staring fearfully at him, as if he might be dangerous.

He ignored her. 'Where's your dog?'

The man said, 'I am here to tell you she dead.'

'Dead?' The young man gave a wild look around him, as though the body were there somewhere. 'I'm sorry. How?'

The man lifted his arm and gestured over the park. The effort tired him. 'Snake bite her and she die.'

The young man could see it happening and feel the empty days stretching. 'You'll miss her,' he said.

'Since puppy,' the man said. He pulled at his shirt. 'When she small I carry her in here. Go everywhere. The difference to me,' he said, holding his arms apart. 'No more she jump on my bed and lick my face, wake up! Time to walk!' He concluded inexplicably, 'She not make the journey to the other side.'

The difference to him. Tears pricked the young man's eyes and the woman on the blanket packed up and hurried away, back to where the world was normal and madmen didn't conjure friends out of the sky.

The others were home when the young man got back to the house. He resented it. They disturbed the peace. He thought about telling them the story of the man and the snake-bitten dog, but changed his mind and felt the old tensions grow.

He woke in the night. He lay still, staring at the ceiling. In the morning he telephoned numbers listed in the yellow pages. It was good to be doing something.

It made more sense to drive his car to the park than to go down on foot. That way he could read a book and keep an eye on the puppy at the same time. Then, when the man was well inside the park, amid familiar surroundings, he would walk in after him and deliver the puppy. Quiet, no fuss, a simple act of unexpected kindness.

It was a fat puppy, coal-black and fluffy. It explored the floor of the young man's car, walking between and under the seats from the rear to the front again, pleased to be alive. It wasn't a bit interested in sleeping on the rags in the cardboard box on the seat. 'Cut it out,' the young man said, laughing, lifting his bare feet off the floor.

His plan was working. The man limped past twenty

minutes later. The young man waited, then followed, catching up to his friend standing on the river bank, watching children cast lines into the water. The air under the trees was cool and dry, perfumed with pine sap.

'He's yours,' the young man said, offering the puppy.

Automatically the man pulled his hands from his pockets, put them back again, and finally stood there, gesturing helplessly. He didn't say anything, and to the young man this was unbearable.

To help him understand what was happening, the young man explained that in a few weeks' time the pup had to be taken back to the dogs' home for a final injection, and that he'd be happy to do that. 'No problem,' he said.

They could stand there like that for ages. It would be best if he eased away quietly now, for the puppy had begun to tremble and yip as if the captive of bad dreams. The young man stepped forward, began to lower the puppy into the dog man's open arms, and noticed a puncture wound in the sorry grey skin of the man's right hand. You'd get a wound like that if you tried to snatch a loved one from a viper's jaws.

He looked at his friend's face, at the kindness in it of someone who has offered a gift, and understood. Then the details dissolved, the young man wrapped the whimpering creature into the warm hollow under his jaw, and the children on the river bank saw a man who has found some love in his life.

POOR RECEPTION

It was the third day of my holiday. My first car, my first holiday without the parents, my last bit of freedom before I started my first job. I'd been driving for about 800kms a day since Melbourne, conscious that I only had another twelve days left. Anyone who had ever driven a car or a truck or towed a caravan was taking the coastal highways of Queensland: it seemed as if the whole country had to start work again in twelve days.

Late January. Sticky, hot days and nights and always the threat of rains and flooding that come at that time of the year in that part of the world. I tried to catch glimpses of the sea, tried to steer clear of the maniacs hogging the road, grew tired and cranky. You'd be cranky too if you'd been going out with someone for eighteen months and you plan a holiday together and at the last minute she tells you that you're too serious and she loves someone else and it's all over.

Then I took a grip on myself. Okay, the holiday wasn't panning out as intended, but there was no reason why I couldn't turn it into something positive. My passion is photography. I had all my gear with me. Since there weren't going to be any happy snaps on the beach this holiday, why not spend time shooting subjects that would test my skill?

That's how I came to take the inland roads. It's a different world out there: remote sheep and cattle stations, old towns, people and places shaped by time, heat and isolation into subject matter for the eye of the lens. I soon felt calmer. I hummed down the country roads in my ancient VW and other drivers actually raised their hands to me instead of running me off the road. There was a country preacher on the radio, casting his vibrant voice out over the land. Sometimes he shouted, but at other times his voice would drop to a whisper, and I blamed it on poor reception until I realised it was simply his way of putting passion into his voice.

I sped past the hitchhiker before I could stop. I had a flashing impression of a young woman, tired and dusty, two duffle bags in the dirt at her feet, giving me a last-chance look. I braked. Watching her in the rear-view mirror, I shifted into reverse. I turned my head to begin backing the car, and that was when the two duffle bags got to their feet and shook themselves. *Dogs.* Big ones. What a bummer. I stopped reversing.

But who would give her a lift if I didn't? Night was coming. Out in the middle of nowhere, anything could happen to her. But how many dogs and hitchhikers can you cram into a VW? Perhaps she was only going a short distance up the road. Or I could take off again.

Too late. Her hot, red face was at my window, puffing, smiling and grateful. She gasped and gulped at me and I shrugged inwardly, accepting that a decision had been made and I couldn't do anything about it. 'Need a lift?' I asked.

'This is great,' she said. 'I'm going as far as you're going. I'm so hot. I'm so *bored.* Really. I couldn't hack it out here another minute. The name's Lisa.'

'I'm going to Cairns,' I said.

She pounded her forehead with the palm of her hand and whooped. 'That's great. Me too.'

Her voice rose to a squeal as I helped her get the dogs (Bramble and Rose) onto the back seat. 'I left Sydney, I don't know, *days* ago. I been on the road one two three *four* days, and I'm really whacked. I thought I'd see some of the country this way, but no one wants to give me a ride, or I get rides with dickheads who hassle me. Totally uncool.'

I opened the boot, pulled a cold beer out of the esky, wiped the butter from it and presented it to her. She sipped it daintily.

'I never drink beer,' she said, 'but it's a hot day, and I have to celebrate, right?'

Finally we set off down the road. She waved her arms and pulled faces as she talked. She seemed to fill the little car. I drove, demure behind the steering wheel, she bubbled over, and in the back her dogs slept and farted.

Cairns. Still a long way down the track. I cleared my throat. 'We've got a fair way to go. Would you be prepared to share the driving?'

'Fine. Just so I get there. I got sixty bucks we can put towards the cost of fuel.'

I shook my head. 'I'm going to Cairns anyway. You don't have to pay me anything.'

'I want to pay my way,' she said stubbornly.

I looked back at the road. 'We'll never make it to Cairns tonight. I've got a tent, a big one. We can share it if you like. That will save on accommodation costs.'

I felt self-conscious as I said it and, without turning my head, I knew that she was giving me an assessing look. I shrugged. 'I wouldn't hassle you or anything.'

'Fine,' she said. There was no expression in it.

She leant back with the knees of her long legs on the dash and started to tell me about herself. 'I've lived all over the place because my dad was in the Air Force. After a while I couldn't hack it.' She ran away a lot, she told me. When she was fifteen she ran away for good. She lived in parks and on the beach, had a string of casual jobs, started to sleep around, got into dope — a life of terrible risks that she'd now put behind her. I think she must have told me everything. Her car and most of her possessions had been stolen a few days before she left Sydney. 'A Honda. I saved all year for that car. Stolen the day after my eighteenth birthday. Bummer. No point in waiting around, but. They've probably stripped it or totalled it by now.'

As she talked, I watched her press the cold beer can to her skin. Her legs and feet were bare and dusty. On her legs and her restless hands there were long, bright scars. She had strong, square hands with short chipped nails. A green ribbon held her hair clear of her face and neck. She touched the scars on her legs. 'I worked in this riding school for a few months.'

After a while she grew listless and stopped talking. When I asked her if she was in a hurry to get to Cairns, she shrugged as if to say no. I began to say a few things about myself but she hunched her shoulders and settled down in her seat, effectively shutting me out. From time to time she turned to hug and kiss Bramble and Rose and murmur endearments to them. Later she fell asleep. I had a feeling of temporariness, nothing new.

In the late afternoon we stopped in a small town so that I could photograph the broad verandahs, the warped weatherboard cottages, the old men yarning on a bench under a peppercorn tree. It took a while, darkness began to settle, and so we decided to buy food and ask for directions to the nearest camping ground. I bought some hamburger meat to fry, but Lisa turned up her nose at it and bought fruit for herself and nuggets for the dogs.

The camping ground was a stony, treeless national park high upon the side of a hill. We pitched the tent and looked down into a valley that winked and changed as the sun set and town lights came on. One or two tiny whirlwinds lifted papers and tossed grit at our legs. There were only a couple of other tents. Everyone else was on the coast road.

I set up the gas burner among some stubby bushes alongside a cement table and bench. The shower block was just across the track from us. As I cooked hamburger meat and drank from a can of beer, Lisa ate apples and bananas and seemed to regain her spirits.

'I was living with this guy in Byron Bay,' she said. 'He's thirty-three and got a wife and two kids, but he wasn't living with them when I met him.' She paused as if to make sense of something. 'Then a few weeks ago he tells me he wants to go back to them, he has to get his head together, etcetera, etcetera, so I split. I thought in Cairns I would stay with my cousin, she lives near the beach, and get a job. If he wants me back again, he knows where to contact me.'

At this point she became confused and unhappy and her eyes filled with tears. I reached out and touched my fingers to her arm.

She jerked away from me. 'I'm all right,' she said. 'You don't have to touch me.'

'Sorry.'

I leant back on the hard bench and gazed at her. It's hard to work out what people want, sometimes. I try to do the right thing and I get my head bitten off.

Lisa looked flushed and unsettled, but then she gathered herself together. 'See, I have to work things out for myself. There's never been anyone else I can rely on. That's why I hate it when people try to invade my space.'

I didn't say anything. *Invade my space.* Was that what I'd been doing?

'Tell me about yourself. You look as if you've got everything together in your life, as if nothing bad's ever happened — whoops, forget I said that, it sounds patronising, I'm sorry.'

I shrugged, as if to say of course I've got everything together, and this is a stupid conversation, and how would you know what I've been through or haven't been through anyway?

I felt old wounds opening up inside me. My girlfriend had accused me of being too serious, as if I had no feelings. How would she know? How would Lisa know? I mean, I have feelings like anyone else, but am I obliged to be emotional all over the place? Getting hassled about this kind of thing twice in two weeks was more than I could take.

I calmed down after a while. I wouldn't be seeing Lisa after tomorrow. We'd pass like ships in the night.

When it was time to crawl into the tent, Lisa made a point of waiting for me to position my sleeping bag before she placed hers in the opposite corner, near the entrance. She brought the dogs in with her. Seeing the expression on my face, she said, 'Well, they'll fret if I leave them outside, and someone might come along and steal them or something.'

'Just so long as they keep still.'

She grinned at me. 'They will if they're not disturbed,' she said.

Great, I thought. Now I'm a sex maniac.

Of course Bramble and Rose were restless all night, keeping me awake with little growls, pacing up and down, stinking the place out. Lisa slept through it all. At one point I had to go outside, and, as I stepped over her, one of the dogs made a rush at me and Lisa woke up with a cry and pushed me away.

'For Christ's sake,' I said. 'I'm only going outside.'

I was standing out there, some distance away, trying to relax and concentrate, when I heard Lisa leave the tent. She didn't seem embarrassed at what I was doing there in the moonlight and even stood nearby and began to talk, more of her dreamy, philosophical rambles about the meaning of life. 'Excuse me,' I said grumpily, and I stalked past her to finish what I'd set out to do in the toilet block across the stony track.

The next morning I woke early and showered away my bad mood. I woke Lisa gently and said that we should be going. 'We've got a full day of driving to get to Cairns.'

She walked across to the shower block, taking the dogs with her, just as the warden drove up to ask for the camping fee. He saw Lisa disappearing into the women's shower block, Bramble and Rose trotting at her heels, and shook his head wearily.

'Mate, mate,' he said. 'You'd better go after the girlfriend and tell her to leave the dogs outside. What if another lady goes for a shower and sees the dogs and dies of a bloody heart attack or something? I could lose my job.'

I paid the fee and walked across to the shower block, wondering how I was going to do this. I stood outside the door and yelled for a couple of minutes but the shower was gushing noisily and Lisa couldn't hear me. I walked in, still shouting. 'Lisa, the warden says no dogs allowed.'

'Damn,' she said. 'You'd better come and collect them.'

She was standing in an open cubicle facing away from me with her hands behind her back, turning slightly one way and then the other to let the hot water stream over her shoulders. She turned her head a little, smiled and pointed to where the dogs sat in a corner. She looked younger and smaller. She had tiny tattoos of red and blue flowers on one thin shoulder-blade. I thought about those flowers on my way back to the car, a dog collar in each hand.

After packing up some of our gear I sat in the entrance to the tent eating a bowl of Raisin Bran and checking my camera gear. Lisa, looking even younger with her wet hair dripping onto a clean shirt, sat opposite me and began to roll a joint.

I offered her the Raisin Bran. 'Want some?'

She gave a small, delicate shudder. 'No thanks,' she said, blowing a wobbly smoke ring out through the tent flap.

Looking happy and renewed, she told me about the beach hideaway where she and her boyfriend had cooked seafood in hot coals in the sand. She smiled and I smiled and snapped her picture. We were sitting cross-legged in the early sun, smiling at each other. It was nice. But then I thought about the little red and blue flowers and something must have passed across my eyes because Lisa suddenly grew wary and began to pack her things. People are always packing up around me.

For the first hour on the road we sat as though in a trance. The air was clean; it let us rush through it with scarcely a sound, and it carried to us the smells of the land. The farmers were going to work; they seemed to nod and wink hello from their utes, and their sons waved as they opened paddock gates. Their kelpies dashed along the fence lines. Later it got much hotter. Lisa drove and I calculated distances, the map balanced on my knees and resting against the dash.

'It'll be late by the time we get there,' I said. 'Do you want to drive straight through?' Part of me wanted her to say we should camp for a second night, part of me wanted to get to Cairns.

'Let's drive straight through,' she said. 'I'm tired of being on the road, you know? We can make it.'

She was a very good driver. She buzzed us past trucks and cars, silent and watchful for hours at a time. We drove through the long day. Lisa talked again when it was my turn to drive. I understood that the things she loved had never lasted long for her. They were taken away or they promised too much and she'd been disappointed. The thing is, this time I listened to her talk about these matters without wanting to groan or roll my eyes or say something snide. She didn't mind when I reached out unconsciously and touched her arm in comfort.

She smiled. 'Maybe you could stay at my cousin's place tonight. That's if you're too tired to keep driving when we get there.'

'Thanks,' I said, smiling back at her. It was better this way, ordinary friendliness without the tension of the other business.

Things began to fall apart at the next town. The fuel gauge was showing empty and we still had another four hours of travelling ahead of us. The town was called Hallett, small, forgettable, with one of everything in the main street: greasy-spoon cafe, general store, post office, bank, garage with a couple of petrol bowsers. The footpaths were deserted. We were the only ones stupid enough to be out in the sun that day.

'Not even a cop shop,' Lisa said. She said it thoughtfully, and I realise now that I should have paid more attention to her tone.

I pulled in and began to fill the fuel tank. Lisa said. 'Don't be cross with me, but I can't pay my share. I lied before. I'm completely broke.'

I smiled. 'That's okay.'

'I hate owing money to people,' she said.

'You don't owe me anything.'

'I'll pay you when I can,' she said.

'Forget about it,' I said, firmly this time.

She fetched water for the dogs, then wandered off. I paid for the fuel, checked the oil and the tyres, washed the windscreen. I stood by the car, taking readings with the light meter so I could take shots of the heat-buckled tar on the footpath. Time went by. Where was she?

At that moment a shop door slammed on the other side of the street and Lisa came out at a run, streaking toward me, shouting, *'Get in. Start the car.'*

I gaped. An elderly man banged through the door of the shop. He looked angry, waving his arms at us.

Lisa piled into the car. *'Drive,'* she shouted.

Infected by her urgency, I planted my foot and sped us onto the road and out of the town. The angry shopkeeper receded behind us, standing on the white line, still shaking his fist.

'What's going on?'

Lisa laughed, a laugh of freedom and triumph. 'Look!'

She waved a fistful of money in my face, tens, twenties and fifties. 'Now I can pay my share.'

'Jesus H Christ,' I said, and I swerved off the road, braking in a cloud of dust. 'Take it back. Immediately.'

The change in her was hard and sudden. 'Are you mad? Do you want to go to prison? Don't sweat it, he'll have insurance.'

I thought about prison, about losing everything. Life had been looking good and now it was turned around 180 degrees. 'Why did you do it?' I asked sadly.

'You need to admit more risk into your life,' she said, poking me. 'Turn things into an adventure like I do.'

'Lisa, it's wrong. What if he took the number of the car?'

She counted on her fingers. 'One, he's old, wears glasses like the bottoms of Coke bottles. Two, you've got interstate plates, hard to remember. Three, your plates are dusty.'

I felt out of my depth. I didn't think she was a bad person, exactly, and I didn't think she deserved to get into trouble with the law, but I did know that she was far ahead of me in life and I'd never catch up. I started the car again and pulled onto the road. 'We'd better cut across to the coastal highway,' I said, 'where we stand less chance of being noticed.'

She was in a teasing mood now. 'I'll make a highwayman of you yet.'

I exploded, all elbows and feet like I am sometimes. '*You're* the one who got us into this mess. I've got a good mind to dump you in the middle of nowhere.'

She looked frightened. She also looked confused and hurt. 'I only wanted to repay your kindness,' she said.

'Having your company was enough, can't you understand that?'

We reached the outskirts of Cairns some time after midnight, passing through the sorts of streets you find in every city, streets where no one seems to go to bed. Cops, taxi drivers, young guys painting and repairing cars in panel-beaters' shops, drunks, kids coming back from the beach. The air was damp with the smells of the sea, the streets were black between the lights.

Lisa's cousin lived in an old wood-frame house on stilts. Palm trees tossed in the sea wind. No one answered the door.

'Not home,' Lisa said. 'Look, I'm sorry but I don't feel right about your staying here without her permission. She's probably at a party or at her boyfriend's place. I'll be okay; I'll sleep on the porch.'

We stood by the driver's door of the VW and she gave me a rueful smile. But I was thinking about the red and blue flowers again. 'You sure? Perhaps we could find a motel, both get a safe night's sleep.'

She smiled crookedly at me. 'I don't think so.'

But then she reached up, pulled my face down and planted a nice big kiss on my lips. 'Loosen up,' she said. 'You know that shopkeeper? I'm going to give him back his money.'

She stepped back so that she could see my face clearly. I felt myself filling with emotion. She touched my cheek. 'It was great meeting you. It was great that you came along. You saved me all kinds of hassles, even if I did nearly give you a heart attack this afternoon.'

I wanted to leave her with some advice as well. One of her dogs was winding around our legs. I reached down, scratched the gentle skull between the ears, felt a strong tail thump against me.

In the end I simply told her to take care. I got into the VW and drove away. I stopped in the next street, though. I parked under a street light to look at the map and, before I could forget them, I wrote down the house number and the street name. It hurt to think that this was the end between us.

I headed north again, hugging the coast, and set up camp on an isolated beach near Port Douglas. All the campgrounds were full; just my luck. The tent seemed empty without Lisa and her dogs. When I awoke the next morning, the remaining days of my holiday seemed to stretch long and hollow before me. I moped about with the camera. I swam in a pool, read, ate fish and chips, but none of those things meant very much to me.

On the third day I read about the murder. The headline was splashed across a local newspaper in a milk bar at Mission Beach. I bought the paper, took it back to my tent, and felt my heart fill with grief as I read it.

She'd been strangled. Police hadn't identified the body, and I hoped it wasn't Lisa, but everything seemed to fit: age, description, possessions — and the most telling point of all, a pair of badly dehydrated dogs standing guard over the body.

I had to know. I couldn't stay on at that lonely beach day after day not knowing. I packed up and headed south again, to Cairns, to the address I'd noted three days earlier.

Lisa's cousin's house was still closed up. There was no sign of Lisa or her things on the screened-in porch. I tried the front door, the back door. Both were locked.

The spare key was under a lump of coral in the rockery and I think Lisa must have found it, too, for when I let myself into the house I found the remains of a snack on the kitchen table.

I also found the note. It was anchored in place with a pepper grinder and read: *Dear Lisa: Gone away till the weekend. Make yourself at home. Someone called Rob phoned (sexy voice!). He said to ring him at the Byron Bay number ASAP. Cheers, Mill.*

My heart started hammering. Her lover had called and she'd gone back to him. She'd hitchhiked and a maniac had picked her up and now she was dead.

But I needed to make sure. I needed to trace her route. I needed to talk to someone, maybe even adopt Bramble and Rose.

According to the newspaper account, the murdered woman had been found near Hallett. I remembered the name — how could I forget it, Lisa streaking across the street toward me with a fistful of stolen money? If the dead woman was Lisa, she was retracing our inland route, intending to return the money. I locked the house, got into the VW and set out on the long journey back.

Lisa waved me down about three hours later, at a crossroads on the kind of stony plain where the sun is always high and scorching, the trees stunted and half dead. There were no other cars on the road, no animals, only the iron roofs of distant houses flashing in the blinding sun.

And it *was* Lisa. She smiled as I slowed the car. The same gutsy manner, the same white teeth, the same brown skin, Bramble and Rose in the dust at her feet.

The car skidded, righted itself, and I stopped and backed up. My grin was wide enough to split my face. My heart felt huge with relief and pleasure.

She wasn't there.

She'd been there and now she wasn't. No place where she could be hiding, nowhere to go, no-one else in sight.

A kind of panic gripped me. I felt cold under that high, hot sun, as though death had found me.

I drove on.

Six times that day Lisa waved me down, grinning, her panting dogs at her feet. Once or twice I took the wrong turnoff, but she always drew me back again.

She was guiding me.

I passed through Hallett, finally. Then, thirteen kilometres south of the town, I saw Lisa for the last time. She was waiting for me at a T-junction, her face alight with anticipation, the face of someone who knows she's heading to the arms of her lover, the face of someone who lives in a world where everything is an adventure.

I stopped a hundred metres short of the junction and watched her for a while. She seemed so happy, swimming in my vision like a mirage. Then out of the haze came a dusty black Land Rover. The man who stepped down from it wore jeans, a grimy white T-shirt, lizard-skin boots, a drooping moustache under his narrow, hooked nose. He helped her load the dogs, helped her load her backpack. I don't know if she sensed two days ago what I was sensing now, the man's mind ticking over, his cruel patience, his knowledge of the back roads. I scribbled his description onto a scrap of paper, a description of the vehicle, the numbers on his licence plates.

Then I drove back to Hallett and that was as far as I got before the police stopped me. So here I am, stuck in a small, airless space, steel bars and razor wire defining my world.

I've told them my story, but they only laugh. Would you believe it? If someone told you that a murder victim came back as a ghost to reveal the identity of her killer, would you believe it? The police laugh when I swear it's true. 'You were seen here in town with the girl a few days ago,' they tell me. 'We've got your description, the girl's description, the description of your car. We've got the dog hairs on the back seat, the girl's fingerprints on everything. What happened? Did you have a fight about something? Did she tell you she didn't want you any more?'

I tell them it wasn't like that, that we were friends. I tell them about the black Land Rover, the man driving it, the number plates.

'That man is a respected member of the community,' they reply. 'Why, he even helped us search the area where the body was found. It does you no good blaming others. You're only reinforcing your guilt.'

I can only hope that Lisa knows I'm here. I can only hope that she's waiting on the back roads at this very moment, sticking her jaunty thumb in the air to someone who will look and listen and understand.

WHERE THE BODIES ARE BURIED

'Maddy Lee. Short for Madeleine?'

Maddy nodded.

'Pretty name,' the woman said.

Maddy said nothing. 'Lee' was okay, but she thought that 'Madeleine' was uncool. Not that anyone called her that: 'Maddy' usually, 'Mad' occasionally. She sat across the desk from the woman and waited. She had her list of questions ready, and fresh batteries in the microcassette recorder. All she wanted to do was complete the interview and go home.

But the woman was in no hurry. Her brown eyes were faintly amused. Maddy stared back defiantly.

The woman had agreed to be interviewed, so why the act?

'Lee . . . Lee,' the woman said suddenly, sharp and assessing now. 'I thought you reminded me of someone. Same bone structure, same slim build. You're Ben Lee's daughter.'

The blood rushed to Maddy's face, hot and unbidden. This was secret, shameful ground, and people were always trampling over it. She lowered her head and muttered non-committally.

'Did he send you here, Maddy?'

The tone was suspicious. 'No,' Maddy said.

'Then why me?'

'I looked in the phone book,' Maddy said. 'Yours was the only agency run by a woman. "Da Costa Investigation Services", according to the listing in the yellow pages. "Ellen Da Costa. Prop".' Maddy looked at Ellen and waited.

Ellen Da Costa relaxed her penetrating stare and smiled. It transformed her face, replacing the habitual scepticism and wariness of her life with sudden warmth. She was in her late thirties, business-like in a slim-fitting dress the colour of autumn leaves. She had striking red hair, heightening the effect of autumn colours, and a strong-willed, passionate face.

'Your assignment is to write a magazine article as part of your TAFE writing course? Are you sure this has nothing to do with your father?'

'Positive,' Maddy said.

'You've inherited his good looks,' Ellen said.

Maddy adjusted her glasses self-consciously. She forced the words out: 'Do you know my father?'

'A little,' Ellen said. 'He was a straight copper, too straight for his own good. That's why corrupt coppers set him up. I quit rather than let that happen to me.'

Maddy leant forward. Ellen had touched on one of the questions on her list. 'You were in the police before you became a private detective? That's where you learnt your skills?'

'Yes.'

'Do you mind if I tape this?'

'Go ahead.'

Maddy positioned the tiny machine between a desk calendar and an ashtray, then switched it on. It looked unobtrusive; with any luck Ellen Da Costa would forget it was there and speak naturally.

'But where did the idea for the story come from, Maddy?'

'In my final year at school we studied crime novels by women writers,' Maddy explained. 'I wrote an essay on the female private eye. I thought why not use that material to compare the life of a fictional private detective with the life of a real one.'

Ellen Da Costa tipped back her head and roared with laughter. 'You want to know if I pack a gun in my knickers, drive a sports car, practice karate, own a cat, sleep with sexy hunks? Maybe I'm bad at housework, a lesbian, the daughter of an aristocrat?' She laughed again. 'Did I cover all the cliches? I've read those books. They're fun to read on a wet Sunday, but that's all.'

She sat there for a while, shaking her head. Maddy waited: this was good stuff.

'Listen,' Ellen Da Costa said, 'I'll tell you about being a female private eye. One, people assume I can't do the job because I'm a woman, so they hire blokes with names like Cliff or Lew. Two, there's nothing romantic or exciting about following someone's philandering husband around or guarding mink coats during Fur Week at the showgrounds. Last night I watched a house for eleven hours straight, drinking thermos coffee and peeing behind a hedge because there was nowhere else to go and I didn't want to lose the person I was tailing. Not exactly Hollywood.'

There was a lively, self-mocking look on Ellen's face. She was enjoying herself. Maddy grinned back. Next question: 'What about special equipment?'

'Special equipment? Look around you.'

Maddy looked. A typewriter, but no fancy radios, listening devices or weapons.

'Not even a computer,' Ellen said. 'Only this old electronic typewriter, which needs a new cartridge every twenty pages. I put all my savings into renting a decent office so that clients will think I'm doing well.' She paused. 'I've been trying to get your father to join me.'

Maddy couldn't let this go unchallenged. 'You must be crazy. His name was in the papers for months: bribery, stealing heroin from the drugs safe at headquarters. TV reporters were camped on our front lawn. Kids gave me a hard time at school. In the end, Mum and I had to move house.'

Ellen's eyes narrowed. 'But charges were never laid against him. He was discharged from the force, but he was never convicted of anything.'

'And the rest,' Maddy burst out. 'Always drunk and abusive. He used to hit us. We don't want to have anything to do with him.'

'Stress, Maddy,' Ellen said quietly. 'Your father knows where all the bodies are buried, and that's a large burden to carry.'

'Bodies?'

'A figure of speech. It means he can name names but he knows if he says anything he'll end up in the harbour.'

A chill crept across Maddy's skin.

'He's stopped drinking, by the way,' Ellen said gently. 'I'm not saying he's a saint, but maybe he deserves a chance?'

Maddy said nothing. She didn't feel ready to see her father again. 'What case are you working on at the moment?'

Instead of replying, Ellen swung around to the typewriter, removed the closely-typed page sitting in it, gathered other pages stacked nearby, and crossed to the safe bolted to the floor under the window. She opened it, tossed in the file and closed the heavy door again.

She returned to her desk. Shutters seemed to have

fallen across her face. 'I don't think you want to know that, Maddy. Now, what else can I tell you?'

But nerves, the stuffy air, and the unwelcome references to her father were getting to Maddy. She badly wanted to splash some water onto her face. 'Is there a bathroom I could use?'

Ellen pointed to a door in the corner. 'In there. One of the perks of having a corner suite.'

Maddy crossed the room self-consciously and shut the door behind her. Somehow, an en suite bathroom didn't fit her image of the tough private eye. They were supposed to work from run-down offices on the wrong side of town, not from a suite in a modern office block. In the foyer downstairs Maddy had seen the list of tenants: accountants, a theatrical agent, a gynaecologist and three import-export agencies. Wednesday, 6 p.m. Everyone but Ellen Da Costa had gone home.

Maddy reached for the flush button. Just as her fingers touched it, she heard voices on the other side of the door.

She froze. More than voices. A muffled scream, sounds of a struggle, bitter male curses: 'You lousy bitch' and 'Sticking your nose in' and 'Open the safe, slag.' There seemed to be four male voices.

Then Ellen, angry, uncowed: 'Get out, Blake.'

A soft cry of pain. They were hitting her. Maddy flattened herself against the wall — as if that would make a difference if they came looking for her. She couldn't breathe.

'Open the safe, I said.'

'All right, if it makes you happy.'

Part of Maddy urged, *Don't give in*, but another part sensed that Ellen had given in to protect them both. Blake and his men would take what they'd come for and leave.

Silence. Then, in quick succession:

'Is this the only copy?'

'Yes.'

'Okay, fellas, do it.'

'No!'

'Is she right-handed? Yes. Fit her hand around the grip. Now, aim it under the jaw. Okay, do it.'

'Blake, please!'

There was a muffled shot.

Maddy drew in a ragged breath, a suppressed wail of pain and terror. She began to tremble. Could those men hear her bones rattling? She wanted to be sick. Breathe in, breathe out, breathe in, breathe out.

'Anything else in there? Tapes, photos?'

'No, boss.'

There was the sound of twin clasps unlocking on a briefcase. 'Shove this stuff in the safe and lock it. If they want a motive for her suicide, this should do the trick.'

'Blakey, what about a note?'

'Not necessary.'

Maddy remembered her father telling her that many suicides failed to leave a note. But thinking of him just now was beside the point. If only those men would leave.

'Oi, Sunshine, where are you going?'

'I need to take a leak, boss.'

An involuntary cry of fear started deep in Maddy's chest. She bit on her knuckles to fight it down.

'Later,' the man called Blake said. 'We can't stick around here.'

Maddy would never forget that voice. It had the rasping quality of gravel on a shovel. She waited. The door to the outer office opened and closed. She slid slowly to the floor, all her strength draining into the cold tiles. She couldn't stay here, but she didn't think she could face what lay beyond the door, either. The only dead bodies she'd seen were on the TV news, and that was enough. They always looked very dead, not like a body in a movie. Maddy began to cry.

After a moment, she stopped. Ellen Da Costa deserved justice, not tears. Maddy got to her feet, pushed the flush button, and edged out into the office.

It wasn't so bad. The swivel chair had been swung around to face the window so that only Ellen's slumped shoulders were visible. Her right arm dangled over the edge of the chair. There was a little pistol on the carpet beneath the lifeless fingers.

Maddy moved to pick up the phone. Then she

paused: What if she got blamed for the murder? Worse, what if the newspapers published her name, and Blake came looking for her? This would have to be an anonymous call.

She wrapped her handkerchief around her right hand, dialled 000, and asked for the police. 'Your name?' the operator said, but Maddy ignored her. She reported the murder, replaced the receiver, and began systematically to wipe every surface she could remember touching since she'd entered the office.

And that's how she remembered the little cassette recorder. It sat there on the desk, tiny red light glowing, tiny motor humming. She snatched it up. *She had the murder on tape.*

Time to go.

The pistol. Maddy hovered indecisively. No: she didn't want to be caught with a murder weapon in her possession.

She took one last look around the office and let herself into the corridor. There were two ways out: an emergency stairwell at one end of the corridor, and the main open staircase halfway along. She'd barely reached the head of the stairs before she heard the street-level glass doors slide open on the floor below and the man she knew as Blake say: 'You two seal off both exits. Ron, come with me. She's still in the building.'

'Right, boss.'

Cold air seeped in with the men. It was dark outside.

A gritty wind had been gusting all day, flinging rain squalls against the windows of the city. Maddy shivered, thoroughly spooked now. What was going on? How did they know?

She ducked through a heavy pneumatic door into the men's toilet. Maybe if they were looking for a female they wouldn't look in here yet. She looked around desperately. No windows. No other doors. Two cubicles. The only way out was up. She was trapped.

Up?

She looked more closely at the ceiling. It was low, constructed of large, lightweight acoustic battens. Maddy imagined the space above, a region of rafters, air-conditioning conduits and sprinkler pipes.

But how?

She clambered onto the sink, then stretched out one foot to a towel dispenser mounted on the side of the cubicle and used it to launch herself on to the top of the cubicle wall. The towel dispenser creaked ominously, but it held. She was balanced half a metre beneath the ceiling. She pushed up with one hand. The ceiling batten moved. She pushed harder. Small particles of plaster and dust fell into her eyes. She kept pushing and the batten finally broke free. She slid it to one side, gingerly inserted her body through the gap, and patted the interior with her hands.

She remembered the tiny torch on her key ring and switched it on. A sturdy rafter stretched along the corridor, with branches on either side over each suite of offices. She would be able to move about freely here and not fall through. Maddy pulled herself into the ceiling, replaced the batten, and sat for a moment to gather her thoughts.

She might be here for hours. Her mother! Her mother would be sure to call the police if she didn't come home soon.

Voices, remarkably close. Blake and another man had come into the Men's.

'Tell me again what the dispatcher said.'

'Anonymous caller, giving this address, reporting someone had been shot, stressing that it was a murder, not a suicide.'

'Jesus Christ.'

'Sounded like a kid, apparently. Female.'

'Unbelievable,' Blake said. 'Just as well we were still in the car park.'

'Just as well they gave us the call, boss.'

Bleakness settled in Maddy. Police. They were police! Even if she got out of here alive, who could she go to? Who could she trust? Maddy fumbled out her cassette recorder and turned it on.

'What next, boss?'

'Finish searching the building. This kid couldn't have got out or we would've seen her.'

The other man sighed. 'It's getting complicated, boss. There are going to be questions about the suicide now.'

'That's why we've got to get rid of this kid.'

Maddy shivered.

'But the Da Costa woman, boss. Now that the body's been reported, we'll have to call in the pathologist and the crime-scene officers.'

'What body?' said Blake confidently.

The other man was clearly puzzled. 'I don't get you.'

'Simple. We cart Da Costa's body away. We report to headquarters that the phone call was a hoax, okay?'

Maddy pictured the grin on the other man's face. 'Good one, boss.'

'We'll dump Da Costa where she'll never be found, like we should have done in the first place. Eventually she'll be reported missing, the stuff we planted in her safe will be found, and everyone will assume she's done a runner.'

Maddy heard a faint, protesting whine and then a click. The tape was full. She put the recorder back in the pocket of her denim jacket.

The men went out. She caught the last bit of their conversation:

'It's seven now. If we don't find her soon, two of us can watch the place overnight and another shift can watch again tomorrow. She's got to come out sometime.'

For the next three hours, Maddy tracked the men as they searched, creeping metres above their heads and trying to remember everything they said. They spent some time in Ellen's office, wrapping up the body and removing it, and it was there that Maddy overheard something that took away her last vestige of hope.

'Check the desk diary. Maybe she had a visitor.'

'Right.' Pages rustled. 'Boss, it says here "Madeleine, TAFE College assignment, 5.30", followed by a phone number.'

'A bloody student. Where was she, the bathroom? We should have checked.'

'Christ, boss, her parents. If she doesn't show up soon they'll report her missing.'

Got you, Maddy thought gleefully. Now you'll have to leave.

'Hello? Is that Madeleine's mother? I'm Ellen Da Costa's associate. She asked me to give you a call . . . no, nothing's wrong. Ellen sends her apologies: she and your daughter have only just started the interview. We thought we should let you and your husband know that Madeleine may be home a little later than expected . . . He doesn't? My apologies . . . You'll see her tomorrow evening? . . . Night duty? . . . Certainly, certainly, I'll pass the message on.'

Maddy heard Blake hang up. Her heart was thudding.

Blake was jubilant. 'Can you believe it? The father doesn't live with them. The mother's just been called to work night duty and doesn't expect to see the kid until tomorrow afternoon. That gives us plenty of time.'

Above them, Maddy suffered. There was no one on

the outside who could help her. She had no way of getting a message out. Anyway, who could she trust? She didn't even know if she trusted herself. She was more of a swot than an athlete. She was no good at skulking in dark places, second-guessing killers.

'Boss, what if we don't find her and she spills everything to people who work here tomorrow?'

'Simple. We show our badges as they arrive and tell them there's a deranged kid in the building. Right, one of you watch the corridor, the rest of you come downstairs with me.'

They went out. Maddy lay on the ceiling beam, thinking things through. Such assurance, such contemptuous indifference. She began to hate the men, not fear them. It galled her to think that a handful of corrupt men could ruin lives — *take* lives — and get away with it.

The least she could do was save Ellen Da Costa's reputation.

Edging carefully through the darkness, Maddy located Ellen's bathroom ceiling and prised out one of the battens. Welcome light flooded her eyes. She was directly above the glass-edged shower stall. It looked strong enough to bear her weight. She eased through the gap.

Once inside the office, Maddy crept to the little safe beneath the window. Of course it was locked. But she remembered something else her father had told her:

too many people took the trouble to install a safe with a combination lock, but then got careless, writing down the combination somewhere nearby in case they forgot it. Good burglars knew all the places. Her father had told her some of the ones he knew, and Maddy started with them.

Nothing. The minutes ticked by. *Think*, Maddy told herself. An ex-cop like Ellen wouldn't have used any of the usual hiding places.

She found herself staring at the push-dial telephone. Ellen had printed the names and numbers for the memory keys on a removable cardboard label held in place by a transparent plastic plate. Five seconds later, Maddy found what she was looking for, a sequence of numbers pencilled on a slip of paper concealed under the memory label.

She'd never opened a safe before. The dial was a silent, sensitive instrument in her hand. She heard a faint click and jerked the door open.

As expected, Ellen's file was missing. There was an empty camera on the bottom shelf, but Maddy was more interested in the items on the top shelf: two clear plastic bags of white powder sealed with paper bands marked with the words 'Drug Squad: Evidence' and a serial number.

Maddy thought of her father and felt a pang of loss and guilt. Ellen was right, he had been set up, presumably by Blake. But if Blake was trying to stop

Ellen, did that mean Ellen was on to him? Had that been the current case she was so secretive about? And what would investigators make of the drugs in Ellen's safe? They'd assume that Ben Lee had been supplying Ellen with drugs he'd stolen from the evidence safe, and arrest him for sure, maybe even accuse him of silencing Ellen.

A hard resolve gripped Maddy. She removed the drugs, locked the safe, returned to the little bathroom. For a moment she considered flushing the drugs away but realised that the men in the corridor might hear her; besides, the drugs were evidence that might be used *against* Blake now.

She paused. Ellen's report would have named the corrupt officers and given dates, incidents and methods. Blake would have burnt it by now, and there were no other copies. But, if Ellen's electronic typewriter was anything like the one Maddy had learnt to type on years ago, there was a way, a painstaking way, to retrieve the lost information.

She returned to the office. Yes! It was a golf-ball typewriter with a nylon ribbon cartridge. The ribbon could be used only once. As each raised letter on the golf ball struck the ribbon, ink was pressed onto the typing paper, leaving behind a blank image of that letter on the ribbon. It was therefore possible to unwind the ribbon and read, character by character, what Ellen had been typing.

Not now, though. Maddy pocketed the cartridge,

closed the lid on the typewriter, hurried back into the bathroom and up into the ceiling again. She stashed the drugs in an air-conditioning shaft, for the packages were too bulky to cart around, but the tape and the ribbon fitted neatly in the pockets of her jacket.

Tape, ribbon, drugs, her own testimony — Maddy had more than enough evidence to put Blake and his friends away forever, vindicate her father and avenge Ellen.

The trouble was, who should she take it to, and how could she get it to them? If Blake caught her first, he'd destroy the evidence, then kill her. She could hide it, but if Blake silenced her it might remain undiscovered for a hundred years. She would have to find a way of reporting to the outside without leaving the building.

She didn't dare use the telephone in Ellen's office. She'd spent too much time there already. She would phone from an office in the far corner of the building.

Regal Marketing had an en suite bathroom similar to Ellen Da Costa's: shower, toilet and a closet with a woman's overcoat and shoes in it. Maddy gulped water gratefully at the sink and made her way into the office. Who should she call? Her father? Too risky: his phone was probably tapped, and he might come barging in to rescue her, risking both their lives. A newspaper, Maddy thought, and a radio station. She picked up the phone.

Dead.

Maddy groaned. Blake would have cut every line to the building.

Just then she noticed a tray on the desk marked 'Outgoing Mail'. It was crammed with same-day delivery courier envelopes, stacked ready to be collected by the courier service in the morning.

Why not? Maddy searched through the drawers, found an unused courier envelope, carefully printed her father's name and address on the label, and placed the cassette tape and the typewriter ribbon inside it. There was no need for a note: the evidence spoke for itself, and her father would take it to someone he trusted. She sealed the envelope, placed it on the bottom of the mail tray, pocketed a packet of biscuits and climbed back into the ceiling. With any luck her father would get the envelope sometime in the morning.

'She's in here. I heard her.'

Maddy stifled a scream. She fitted the acoustic ceiling batten into place just as doors burst open beneath her.

'Sorry, boss. I could have sworn I heard something.'

'Little bitch. We'll get her.'

After a minute of opening and closing cupboard doors, they went out again.

Time to rock the boat. Time to push *their* buttons for a change.

Maddy crept along the corridor to the cleaners' storeroom, dropped down into it, and unlatched the door. She set fire to a bundle of rags, paper and cleaning solvents with Ellen's matches, and when acrid smoke began to rise, she climbed back into the ceiling, replaced the batten and hurried away from the storeroom. She could hear water in the pipes: the automatic sprinklers had come on, which meant a fire alarm must be sounding somewhere.

A couple of minutes later she heard a distant siren wailing mournfully through the night. It came closer. Another siren sounded, and another. She heard the trucks pull up, she heard running footsteps, she heard voices.

'Who the hell are you?'

'It's okay, fellas, we're police.'

'What's the story?'

'We had a report of vandals. Probably scarpered by now.'

'Well, the fire's out. No damage. We'll be off.'

'Sorry you boys got called out,' Blake's voice replied, an edge of venom in it.

Maddy grinned. She was no closer to getting out, but she had succeeded in rattling Blake's cage, as her father would say.

Maddy stayed all night in the ceiling. She consumed half of the biscuits, stretched out on a beam and slept fitfully until dawn. She didn't want to risk further guerilla tactics: if she kept quiet from now on, Blake might think she'd somehow slipped away from the building in all the confusion.

A clanking bucket woke her. Disbelieving voices. Cleaners. They'd discovered the fire in the storeroom.

Maddy thought about the next stage. People would be coming to work soon, well dressed, smelling of soap and shampoo. They'd greet one another, sit behind their desks, make phone calls, brew coffee. If she were to drop in on them unannounced from the ceiling, they'd call the police before her feet hit the floor and wouldn't believe a word she said. She felt dirty, smelly and scruffy. Just then she would have given anything to soak in a hot bath.

First things first. The only thing that would get her out of the building was a convincing disguise. Blake was looking for a kid, and that's exactly what Maddy looked like: jeans. T-shirt, denim jacket, runners, long straight hair. The only sophisticated thing about her were her glasses with their slim French styling. How could she add to that effect?

She remembered the overcoat and shoes in the closet at Regal Marketing, and crept back along the rafters and dropped into the little bathroom. Her arms ached. She didn't know how much longer she'd be able to keep this up.

She opened the closet. There was a scarf with the coat. The shoes were slender black court shoes. She hoped she wouldn't have to run in them, or she'd snap her ankles.

Voices in the corridor outside. Keys rattling. Someone was arriving for work.

Maddy tossed the clothing into the ceiling space and pulled herself in after them, dislodging a fine dusting of plaster onto the sink beneath her. Too bad. With any luck they'd think the cleaners had been careless.

She waited until mid-afternoon before dropping into the women's room in the main corridor. She dressed rapidly in one of the cubicles, first stripping down to her underwear then pulling on the overcoat, tucking the scarf around her throat and stepping into the elegant shoes.

She hobbled out of the cubicle, stuffed her clothes under paper towels in the rubbish bin, and examined herself in the mirror. Almost convincing at a quick glance. Anyone would think she had a dress on under the coat, though they might wonder why she wasn't wearing tights.

Her hair. She plunged her hands in the deep pockets to think about that and her knuckles brushed against a couple of wiry shapes in the bottom. Hair clips!

Working swiftly now, Maddy coiled her hair at the back of her neck and pinned it to the top of her scalp. This was one time she didn't curse having thick, heavy hair. She shook her head experimentally and the roll stayed in place.

Very sophisticated. It was remarkable how much older she looked. No make-up, but plenty of women don't wear make-up.

She sauntered out into the corridor. It was empty. She didn't expect to see Blake or his men in the building itself, but they would be out there somewhere, watching the exits.

But her image wasn't quite complete. She needed to carry something: a briefcase, a folder, even a magazine.

She wandered into the theatrical agency's waiting room. There were photographs of second-rate actors pinned to the walls and a scatter of showbiz magazines on a coffee table next to an armchair.

A young man looked over his glasses at her. 'Help you?' It was a snooty voice; it seemed to stick its nose in the air.

'I'm looking for work,' Maddy said. 'Stage or screen —'

'Sorry. Our books are full.'

'Oh.'

The young man turned to answer the phone. Maddy snatched up a glossy magazine and went out.

She paused for a moment at the sliding glass doors on the ground floor. A perfectly ordinary-looking street outside: cars, taxis, cyclists, a milk-bar, a bellowing bus, an old man rummaging for aluminium cans.

Where was Blake?

Maddy took a deep breath and left the building, and, as she walked, she had a sense that all life was concentrated on this footpath, on these steps she was taking one by one. She felt the weight of the world pressing down. It wouldn't let up until she was with someone she trusted.

The voice was a low, chilling growl behind her. 'Hello, Madeleine.'

A hand grasped her elbow. Something hard pressed against the base of her spine. 'If you make a scene, I'll shoot you.'

'What's going on?' Maddy spluttered. 'Who are you?'

Blake jerked her arm. 'Don't give me that crap. We noted the appearance of every person who entered the building this morning. You weren't one of them.'

A car braked at the kerb. There were two men in the front seat, another in the back. Blake bundled her into the car.

'Boss,' the driver said, 'I don't like it.'

'Just drive.'

'The radio, boss. I've been monitoring the police band but all transmissions stopped two minutes ago. It's eerie.'

It was then that Maddy noticed how quiet the street had become. No vehicles passed them. There were no pedestrians about, only the old man, and he had his arm deep in a rubbish bin.

Blake noticed it, too. He swore bitterly.

Maddy craned her head. Men in padded blue jackets were swiftly placing barriers at both ends of the street. Police cars had pulled in behind the barriers.

A man wearing plain clothes raised a loudhailer to his lips. 'Let her go, Sergeant.'

Blake swore again. He said to the others: 'We can bluff this out.'

'How, boss? It's obvious they're on to us.'

'Shut up. Let me think.'

The loudhailer snapped again: 'Sergeant Blake. Serious allegations have been made against you and your men. You are ordered to let your hostage go and surrender immediately.'

'They know, boss.'

'Do what you like,' Blake said viciously. 'The bitch is my ticket out.'

He pushed Maddy out of the car ahead of him, then held her around the waist, the gun barrel angled under her jaw. He shouted, and Maddy felt his spittle spray her neck and ear. 'I'm leaving and I'm taking her with me.'

Maddy trembled. She could feel her energy slipping away.

Until a voice said softly: 'Maddy, love.'

The old wino didn't look so old or derelict any more. He looked loose-limbed and dangerous, a revolver in his hand, a police ID clipped to his top pocket. For a brief moment Maddy's father acknowledged her with a flicker of shame and apology, a look that hardened as he turned to Blake and said, 'Let her go.'

Blake swung around. 'You,' he snarled. 'I thought I'd finished you for good.'

Maddy's father shook his head. 'Someone finally listened. My daughter's evidence clinched it.'

'What evidence?' Then, 'If she's your daughter, you'll do anything to get her back, right?'

Maddy's father ignored him. 'Maddy, remember what I said about getting mugged?'

Maddy remembered. At once she lifted her foot and drove it hard towards the ground, raking the sharp heel down Blake's shinbone and into the soft toe of his shoe.

Blake screamed. His grip relaxed. Before he could tighten it again, Maddy twisted free of his arm and threw herself to the ground.

At the same moment, her father charged, driving his shoulder into Blake's stomach. Blake collapsed, his gun clattering onto the pavement. Then other men rushed in and the footpath erupted into unnerving shouts and scuffles as Blake and his men were shoved face down and handcuffed.

Gentle hands helped Maddy to her feet. 'You okay?'

She looked searchingly at her father's face. The burden of their unhappy past was there in his eyes. She smiled. 'I'm fine.'

He nodded, relieved, and stepped back from her as if uncertain what to do next.

Maddy solved that. She touched her father's arm. A lot had changed, and there were things she couldn't forgive, but that didn't mean the connection between them had to be bad now, only different.

Maddy's father grunted. [illegible] remember what I said about getting muddled?'

Maddy concentrated. At once she lifted her foot and drove it hard towards the ground, [illegible] down Blake's sandshoe and into the soft [illegible] of his ankle.

Blake screamed. His grip relaxed. Before he could [illegible] it again Maddy twisted [illegible] out of his grasp and threw herself to the ground.

[illegible]

[illegible] Blake [illegible] the footpath [illegible] Blake and his mates [illegible] down and [illegible].

[illegible] Maddy [illegible] 'You okay?'

[illegible]

He nodded, relieved, and [illegible] back [illegible] as if [illegible].

Maddy smiled back. She touched [illegible] arm. A lot had changed, and there were things she couldn't forgive, but that didn't [illegible] on the [illegible] of [illegible] them back to [illegible] had been, only different.

BLAME THE WIND

Picture this: I was small, thin and secretive; Carl was tall, strong and open. I was tongue-tied around girls; Carl was dashing and successful. I was full of doubts and scruples; Carl went ahead and took what he wanted. I was fifteen; Carl was sixteen. I had disliked him for all of my life; he scarcely considered me one way or the other. People thought the sun shone out of him, they said he could do no wrong; when they looked at me their eyes would glaze over. But one night he was undone by a ghost and I saw his feet of clay.

Carl and I are cousins. Our mothers are sisters, close and loving. His father owns a sprawling sheep station, mine edits the weekly *Chronicle* in the nearby town, and the two families meet for Christmas, Easter, long weekends — in fact, any opportunity they can find.

This time it was different. This time Carl and I were to be alone together. Our parents had tickets to see *The Phantom of the Opera* and since the city was five hours away by road, they had decided to make a weekend of it.

'Just think,' my mother said. 'No adults around for two whole days. You'll have a great time together.'

'Yeah, great,' I said sourly.

'Auntie Kay has cooked your lunches and dinners. All you have to do is heat them up.'

'Can't I come with you? Carl can play with his horse for two days.'

My mother looked at me sharply. 'Sarcasm is not appealing, Robert.'

Sarcasm was my only defence against Carl in those days. I liked to think it was the tactic of a clever person. No one ever appreciated it.

'So that's settled then,' my mother said, and an hour later Carl and I were waving our parents off from his verandah.

The homestead is called Caltowie, a long, low, cool house made of local stone, set among sheds, fruit trees and stunted palms in the foothills of a range of stony hills. The verandah looks out over a vast blue–grey plain dotted with sheep and clumps of mallee scrub. It is red dirt country. Dusty tracks scribble across the flats. The blue horizon floats in the distance; willy-willys spin grit and grass into the hot sky; there is ancient rock art in secret gullies. It is a harsh, beautiful place.

I watched the car recede until it was swallowed up by the horizon. I could see the tin roofs of the town far away. I thought longingly of my bedroom there, my books and tapes.

'We bought another property,' Carl announced.

Uncle Bert was always buying more land. Soon they'd own Australia. 'Really?' I said.

Carl nodded importantly. 'Let's camp there tonight.'

I sighed. All I wanted to do was disappear with a book, but I'd done that to him once before, when I was ten, and had never been allowed to forget it. 'Is it far from here?'

Carl waved his hand vaguely at a region of scrubby hills. 'Hour and a half.'

'On our bikes?'

Carl looked at me pityingly. 'Don't be stupid. We'll take the Land Rover.'

'Are you allowed to?'

His face grew heavy with cunning. 'What the oldies don't know won't hurt them.'

I shrugged. Carl knew how to drive, of course. He could do anything.

'There's an old house we can camp in,' Carl went on. 'We'll take sleeping bags, the camping stove, the metal detector.'

Now I was interested. I loved roaming along dry creek beds with the metal detector. We'd never found gold, but we once found a knife blade and a rust-pitted rifle barrel. 'Sounds good,' I said.

'We'll go at six, after the oldies have rung us.'

I groaned inwardly. It was only ten o'clock in the morning. Eight hours of Carl's idea of fun — drinking Uncle Bert's whisky, shooting galahs, arm-wrestling matches, chain smoking, sexual boasting, and all the time hearing him call me a wimp.

We did all that, and more. The highlight for Carl was interrupting CB radio conversations between truck drivers on the distant Broken Hill road. 'Ten-four, rubber duckie,' he'd say. 'The cops are on your tail. You've spilt your load. Your back wheel's fallen off.' Then he'd cackle, and the drivers would curse. When he got bored with that, he called me a wimp. 'Hey, wimp. Ever done it with a girl? Ever stolen anything?'

Our parents rang that evening, we yacked for ten minutes — yes, Mum, no, Mum — and then loaded the Land Rover and set off. The track was rough, but that didn't stop Carl from driving like a maniac. Kangaroos had begun to materialise for their evening feed, but Carl didn't notice. We almost hit one before he slowed to a safer pace.

We arrived just as the sun was setting. I was glad: the road had bruised my tailbone, my nerves were bad from Carl's driving, and I was tired of opening and closing a million gates between Caltowie and the abandoned farmhouse.

Carl pulled up and turned off the engine. We sat for a moment, eyeing the house. It was dark and squat, the windows fiery red in the last rays of the sun. Those red windows were like blood-flecked eyes watching us. There were no trees nearby, no shrubs or flowers. The stony ground was baked hard from centuries of the sun's heat. To one side of the house was a rotting log barn, as dry and bare as a ribcage in the dust. We sat there, having second thoughts. The Land Rover snapped and ticked around us as the engine cooled.

'Hey!'

Carl's voice was indignant. Surprised, I looked at his face. He was pointing a quivering finger at the house. 'Look!'

I looked. The door was opening. A figure appeared. It was a young woman, her face shadowy. She stood there watching us.

'The place is meant to be empty,' Carl said. His face had changed from fearful white to its normal angry red. 'She's trespassing.'

'Maybe she's lost,' I said, looking around doubtfully. I couldn't see a car or a bike anywhere. Had she walked here?

'I'll soon find out,' Carl said, slamming his door. He strode across the dusty yard. I followed him. We stopped a couple of metres from the young woman.

'You're trespassing,' Carl said. 'This is my land.'

She said nothing, but regarded us solemnly. Then she

smiled and my heart turned over. So did Carl's, I think. It was a beautiful face, and a smile that put you at the centre of things.

'I'm sorry, I didn't know it had new owners,' she said. Her voice was low, unflustered, a pleasant growl.

Carl swelled importantly. 'My dad bought it recently.'

There was that smile again. I saw that she was young, our age, maybe a bit older. 'My name is Anna Mead,' she said.

Carl was baffled. 'Mead? That's the name of the people who used to live here.'

Anna nodded. Wings of glossy black hair fell across her cheeks. 'Distant relations,' she said. For just a moment then, a twist of bad memories seemed to cloud her eyes.

'How did you get here?' I asked.

She gestured vaguely. 'I was given a lift.'

'Are you alone?'

She nodded.

'But why are you here?' Carl demanded.

Anna inclined her head, indicating a rocky bluff some distance away. 'The rock art has fascinated me since I was little.'

'Well,' Carl said, looking at me and then at the girl again, 'I suppose it's all right. But we want to camp here tonight.'

'It's your place,' Anna said.

Carl smiled expansively. 'We'll share.'

Anna helped us to gather our gear and we entered the gloomy kitchen, the only habitable room left standing. She lit candles and at once the walls and ceiling seemed to close in on us. I saw a floor of packed dirt, a crumbling fireplace, a rickety wooden cupboard and very little else. There was no sign of Anna's things. I guessed she'd stacked them in the cupboard.

Then I gathered wood, made a fire and emptied tins of stew into a saucepan. I was being tactful. I could sense a current of attraction running between Carl and Anna. He'd taken her into the shadows, and I could hear her soft murmurs and his voice, lower and deeper. It was a situation I was used to. Carl always got the girl.

As I watched the stew heat up I thought about the situation, trying to read between the lines. According to Carl, the Mead property had been abandoned for years. Neighbours looked after it, in return for grazing rights. They never saw anyone from the Mead family. Everything was conducted by letter. But someone must have died finally, for trustees stepped in and put the property on the market, and Uncle Bert bought it.

But that didn't explain Anna Mead. I imagined her as a little girl, visiting the property, an uncle taking her out to see the rock paintings. It wouldn't be something she'd forget.

Then she laughed softly. I couldn't help it, I had to turn around to see what they were doing. Carl had his arm around her waist. He was nuzzling at her ear. She twisted away, a slender shape in old-style jeans and a plain cotton shirt, expertly avoiding his wet lips.

Carl saw me and grinned broadly. 'Hey, dude, how's it goin'?'

His jokey American accent was another thing I hated about him. I looked away. 'Dinner's almost ready.'

'Far out, man.'

I pulled three old packing crates into a circle around the fire and served our meal. Carl and Anna used the enamel plates, I ate from the saucepan. 'This is the life,' Carl said, grinning, nudging Anna. Whenever he did that it generally meant he was feeling very sure of himself.

The billy began to boil. 'Tea?' I asked.

'How about some firewater, dude?'

With dismay I watched Carl fish around in his pack and bring out a bottle of Uncle Bert's whisky. 'Not for me,' I said.

'Aaah,' said Carl disgustedly. He nudged Anna. 'The guy's a wimp, a nerd.'

Anna glanced at me sympathetically. Then she smiled at Carl, melting his heart. 'No thanks.'

Carl shrugged. 'No sweat. All the more for old Carl.'

He tipped the bottle. The liquid glugged into his throat.

Then someone's fingernails screeched across the window glass outside.

My heart clenched. I glanced up. I couldn't see

anything. Carl looked foolish, the bottle a couple of centimetres from his lips. The blood had drained from Anna's face, leaving her pale and tense.

'What was that?'

Carl recovered first. He gestured carelessly. 'The wind.'

It's true, a wind had risen outside. I imagined it hurling twigs and dust at the house. But it had sounded exactly like fingernails on glass.

Carl narrowed his eyes comically and looked at Anna. 'Believe in ghosts?'

'Maybe.'

He edged closer, putting his arm around her. She seemed to fit herself against him and they both looked at me. I glanced away. It felt to me like two against one.

'Let's scare young Robert,' Carl said.

I stared at the floor, avoiding the leer I knew had come on to his face.

'Let's freak him out with ghost stories,' he went on. 'Anna, you go first.'

'All right.' Her voice was soft in the darkness. The candlelight seemed to shift. 'This is a true story.'

'Ha! Everyone says that.'

'This is a true story,' she went on, ignoring him. 'A family was driving along a lonely road at night. There were hardly any towns, only isolated houses set back far off the road. It got later and later. They came to a railway crossing. There were no signals operating, so they slowed down and began to cross. Suddenly a train appeared. They hadn't heard it and there were no lights on it. They got across just in time.'

She stopped.

'So?' Carl demanded.

'So the line had been closed for years. There shouldn't have been a train on it. They found out later that a family was killed at that level crossing twenty years earlier.'

One of Carl's techniques with girls was to scoff at them. Amazingly, they seemed to like it. He tried it with Anna. 'You call that a ghost story?' He swayed sideways, bumping his shoulder against hers, and peered at his bare arm. 'That story didn't even raise goosebumps.'

Anna smiled at him. Encouraged, he turned to me. 'Rob, your turn.'

'This is also a true story.'

'Yeah, yeah.'

'A man was driving home very late at night along a lonely road —'

'Always a lonely road at night,' said Carl snidely.

'Suddenly he felt chilled to the bone. He couldn't work it out. Then he happened to glance in the rearview mirror and saw a man sitting in the back seat. He turned around, but no one was there; he looked in the mirror, and saw the man. He screeched to a halt, got out of the car, and ran. It turned out that a hitchhiker was murdered on that part of the road a year earlier.'

'Weak,' Carl said. He was sitting as close to Anna as

he could get. His arm was around her waist. She was leaning against him, staring dreamily into the coals.

'Do better,' I said.

'Right.' He dropped his voice and hunched over in a parody of fear and dread. 'A honeymoon couple was driving across the moors late at night. The wind howled, it was wet and misty, they were the only people about. To cheer themselves up they listened to the radio. There was a news item about a mass murderer who had escaped from the asylum. About four o'clock in the morning, the car broke down.'

Irritation rose in me. 'Everyone knows this story. It's been told a million times before.'

'Shut up. The car broke down, so the husband set out to fetch help. He was gone for hours. The wife was getting more and more nervous. She had all the doors locked and had the radio on. Suddenly . . .'

Carl paused dramatically. Anna cuddled against him, shivering with delighted fear. I looked away sourly.

'Suddenly,' Carl said, 'she heard a thumping sound on the roof. She didn't dare get out. She just sat there. Luckily, after a while she saw policemen coming towards her out of the mist.'

Carl stopped again, but this time it wasn't for effect. His face went tense in the firelight. Anna was also looking spooked. Someone had just scraped a stake of some kind against the wall outside. Fear made Carl's voice wobbly. 'What was that?'

I got up. 'I'll have a look.'

For some reason I wasn't feeling frightened, only annoyed that Carl had taken his story from a book. I stood outside listening. The wind had dropped to a hollow moan in the mallee scrub. The Land Rover gleamed dully in the moonlight. I circled the house twice. Nothing, not even a loose wire or a flapping branch. I went back inside.

'Well?'

I shrugged. 'Blame the wind. A tumbleweed probably scraped along the wall.'

Carl didn't look convinced. He took another swig from the whisky bottle. 'Anyhow,' he said after a while, 'the girl in the car saw the cops stop some distance away. They wouldn't come any closer. Instead they beckoned to her. She got out. "Quick," they said. "Run hard and don't look back." So she ran and she was rescued.' He paused. 'The trouble was.' he said, 'she looked back.'

He folded his arms complacently. Anna moved away from him and stared at his face. 'You can't stop the story there,' she said.

He grinned. 'I suppose you want to know what she saw.'

He waited, drawing out the tension. 'She saw the escaped maniac on top of the car, banging her husband's head on the roof.'

Anna wailed, 'That's horrible.'

Carl sniggered. 'Thought you'd like that one.'

'You're mean,' she said. 'Also, that's not a ghost story, it's a horror story. I'll give you a proper ghost story.'

Carl rolled his eyes exaggeratedly, hoping to make her laugh. He used to say to me, 'Make 'em laugh and you're halfway to home base.'

'Do you want to hear it or not?' Anna demanded.

'Shoot, darlin',' Carl said.

Anna's voice grew low and throaty, taking on a quality of great sadness. 'There was a girl deeply in love with a boy.'

'Love story,' said Carl in an ugly voice, winking at me.

Anna ignored him. 'It was the summer holidays and they got permission to go camping with another boy. But this other boy was secretly in love with the girl. He began to make life unbearable for them, trying to separate them, trying to sneak kisses, saying insulting things about her boyfriend. He was insanely jealous. It got so bad they took off one night and found an empty house where they could be alone together.'

Carl sniggered. 'No prizes for guessing what they got up to.'

'But the jealous one followed them. They blocked the doors and windows but he fought his way in.'

Anna stopped then, as if to listen, but the world outside was silent, still.

'What happened?' I asked.

'The most devastating thing — her boyfriend turned

out to be a coward. He ran away. The jealous one got in, and said if I can't have you no one can, and murdered her.'

'What happened to him?'

'He later killed himself.'

'That's not a ghost story either,' said Carl scornfully.

'Oh but it is.' Anna lifted her head and looked long and hard at him. 'They say her spirit remains restless, looking for a brave lover. She'll never be at peace until she finds him.'

Carl's face twisted in disgust. 'I've heard nursery rhymes scarier than that.'

Anna wrapped her arms about herself for comfort. She began to rock gently. Carl, realising he wasn't going to win her with jokes and teasing, slid his arm around her. We were silent. We stared at the flames. Some time later I was aware of Carl leading Anna to a corner of the room. I heard whispers and soft fabricky sounds. They were sitting on the floor, his unfolded sleeping bag around their shoulders and over their knees. I wasn't surprised. I watched the coals grow dim.

Then the noises returned. This time there was no mistaking them, a series of angry scrapes against the wall outside. Carl stood up, his face pinched with fear. 'Rob, was that you?'

I ignored him, trying to track the sound. It went along one wall, turned the corner and continued. It went right around the house. Then silence.

I took out my pocket-knife and opened the blade. In my other hand I held the torch like a club. 'I'm going to see what it is.'

I don't know why I did it. Because Carl had shown fear? Because Anna was there? Because I like to think there are concrete explanations for everything? Whatever the reason, I went outside, scouted around for five minutes, sensed a presence of someone or something, but saw nothing.

I went back inside. I saw their faces peering at me, pale and tense in the firelight. I tried to be soothing. 'The damn wind,' I said.

Carl looked unconvinced. Anna, on the other hand, was distressed and agitated, as though private demons were closing in on her. 'Don't leave me,' she said suddenly.

No one had said anything about leaving her.

'Try to get some sleep,' I said.

'What about you?'

'I'll sit up for a while.'

In truth, I wasn't tired. I also thought that someone should stay alert, just in case, but I didn't tell them that.

I was dozing when the sounds started again. Knocks this time. Exactly like a demented fist demanding entry. The door vibrated, shaking dust from the cracks. The windowpanes rattled. The fist went around the house, pounding on the walls.

I date Carl's disintegration from that point. He tossed aside the sleeping bag and scrambled to his feet. He shrank back against the wall, heard the fist strike it near his heart, and stumbled toward the fire. He seemed smaller, holding himself in, bowed down, his body shaking terribly. 'That's no wind. That's no wind,' he said. He tipped back his head and screamed at the presence on the other side of the wall. 'Go away! Leave us alone!'

In answer, the fingernails screamed down the glass again. A stake, something sharp, scraped the walls. Then I pictured an effortless leap in the darkness, for heavy feet began to march up and down on the roof.

Carl cried out, but it was Anna who got my attention. Her agitation was more pronounced. She seemed to be consumed with dread. Her hands went over her eyes and she moaned, 'Don't leave, don't leave.'

Somehow I didn't think she meant Carl. Not that Carl was any help. He grabbed the torch, pulled the door open and disappeared into the night. A few seconds later I heard the Land Rover. Headlights swept across the window. He was gone.

I closed the door. I crossed the room. I knelt next to Anna, reached out, and gently took her hands from her eyes. She looked at me searchingly. 'Don't leave.'

'I won't.'

I'd never been in a girl's arms before. Anna's seemed to wrap me in silk, almost real, almost a dream. The presence outside grew frenzied, rattling the bones of the old house, but our fear was gone. We were lost in each other.

At daybreak the fury stopped. Anna made a curious sound, like an immense sigh after endless torment. I watched her sleep. Her face changed subtly, peace taking the place of strain.

I must have slept then, for I remember hearing a vehicle and jerking awake to find myself alone. I went outside. Carl had returned. He was facing Anna on the hard ground between the house and the Land Rover, his hands on her hips, talking to her in his intense way, the way that always worked for him. It was like a fist striking me, seeing that.

But I needn't have worried, for Anna backed away from him. Her movements were calm; her smile gave nothing away. She began to walk to the track that led away from the house. I guessed where she was going — to see the rock art in the wind-carved cliffs at the rear of the property.

Carl hurried alongside her. There was something sheepish about him, something sly and unappealing. He'd behaved badly, and now he thought he could atone for it. 'I had to do it,' he said.

She didn't respond.

'I went to fetch help,' he insisted. 'Rob's useless, he's a wimp, so I knew I'd have to be the one.'

No response. I didn't respond either. We all knew

it was a lie. It would always be there between us. He would always be diminished by it.

I spared him one thing. As Anna moved away. Carl followed her for a short distance, trying uselessly for a look, a smile. The thing is, they passed between me and the house, where the old windows were like mirrors. I saw the reflection of the Land Rover, the distant scrubby trees. I saw myself, calm and watchful. I saw Carl, his weakness and shame.

The thing is, I didn't see Anna. Anna didn't register in the glass.

If you care to search for it, the story is in old files at the *Chronicle* office. I had to go back forty years, to the 1950s. It's essentially as Anna told it. They were friends, two boys and a girl, holidaying at the farm belonging to the girl's elderly uncle. They must have had a falling out. The uncle came back from town and found the bodies. It broke his spirit. He never lived there again.